ISTANBUL ICARUS

AN INTERNATIONAL DETECTIVE THRILLER

LUKE RICHARDSON

1

Uludağ, Turkey. Ten years ago.

Ahmed Sadik peered out through the windscreen of his classic Alfa Romeo. The curving mountain road of Uludağ stretched out before him, tantalizing him to go faster. On one side of the road, the snow-covered slopes of the mountain rose towards the sky. On the other side, they fell steeply away.

The snow was bright and crisp. Sadik wondered whether it had fallen recently. Having lived three hours' drive away in Istanbul for most of his life, Sadik only remembered visiting the mountain once or twice. He rolled down the window and cold air whipped into the car. The balmy streets of Istanbul seemed like another world when compared to out here.

Sadik applied pressure to the accelerator, and the Alpha's engine rose from a purr to a grumble. With the window open, the noise reverberated from the mountain. Sadik loved the sound of this old car. At the right speed, and on the right road, it felt as though it became a living thing.

Sadik glanced through the side window. A few feet away, a metal barrier flickered past. Beyond the barrier, the only break in the pearlescent snow was a collection of trees—just icy brushstrokes from here—two hundred feet below. This high on the mountain slopes, these roads could be icy, too. Sadik applied the brake gently. The powerful machine obeyed, somewhat reluctantly.

He slowed further and cruised around a narrow bend, ice and gravel cracking beneath the tires.

Sadik indicated and pulled into a single-track road. The Alfa's powered rear wheels slipped for a moment. The car fishtailed left and then right. Sadik reduced the pressure on the accelerator. When the car was back under his control, he accelerated again, keeping the car within the worn tire tracks. Experience had taught him that sometimes the best progress was slow and steady. Speed often came with danger not far behind.

Sadik pulled up outside a wooden cabin and killed the engine. Thick snow blanketed the cabin's roof and a thread of smoke curled from the chimney. Warm light radiated from the windows on either side of the door.

Sadik exited the car and looked up at the sky. It was already getting dark, and here, far from the light pollution of the city, stars shimmered across the heavens.

"Mr. Sadik." A voice came from the door of the cabin. "Thank you for making it all this way to see me."

Sadik looked around at the cabin. He recognized the figure of Esin Kartan, the only woman on his executive team and the reason he had traveled from the city. Esin leaned against the cabin's door frame and beckoned him in. She was impeccably dressed, with her hair styled in her trademark precision bob. Warm light streamed out around her and patterned on freshly fallen snow.

"It's my pleasure." Sadik climbed the stairs leading up to the cabin. Snow crunched beneath his shoes. "It's nice to get out of the city and let her stretch her legs." He nodded at the Alfa Romeo.

"She is a beauty," Esin replied. "We don't get many sports cars up here. Once the temperature drops, they're more trouble than they're worth on the mountain roads."

Sadik nodded. "I'll be back down before that." He glanced again at the sky. "Either way, I'll be fine. These European-made cars are tough as tanks."

"Of course. Come in, come in."

Sadik followed Esin inside the cabin. He scrutinized the younger woman, moving ahead with her normal calm and grace. During their phone call the previous day, she'd sounded uncharacteristically worried, almost frantic. Concerned, he had promised on the spot to make the long journey out to see her today. If one of his team had a problem, Sadik had a problem. He looked after his team and they looked after his company.

Sadik glanced around. The cabin was small but cozy with wooden walls and a fire cracking in the grate. Two large sofas in deep red looked as though they could swallow a man whole.

"Can I get you a drink? I have wine, or perhaps a whiskey?" Esin strode towards a cabinet on the far side of the room.

"No thank you, Esin," Sadik replied calmly. "You know I don't drink. I haven't touched a drop in nearly twenty years."

"Yes, of course, my apologies." Esin turned and smiled. Sadik caught her eye. "A tea perhaps? I have just the thing."

Sadik replied with a single nod and lowered himself onto the sofa by the fire. He stared into the hearth as the flames crackled and flared. The rumbling of a boiling kettle floated through from the kitchen.

"I can only ever find this beautiful tea in Antalya," Esin said, pacing back from the kitchen with a china cup in one hand. "Whenever I visit, I buy a bag or two."

Sadik accepted the steaming cup and placed it on the table beside him. He leaned forward and placed his hands on his knees.

Esin sunk gracefully into the opposite sofa.

"Tell me what's bothering you?" Sadik asked, his eyes meeting hers. "It must be really important if it couldn't wait until next week."

Esin cradled the cup in her hand and returned Sadik's gaze. She cleared her throat and then took a sip from the cup.

"It's about the company, sir. I wanted to talk with you about your plans for Sadik-Tech's future."

"Okay..."

"I needed to do it privately. It's important we maintain a united front, isn't it?"

"Yes, it is, of course. You know my door is always open to you. We can talk about anything."

"I'm worried about some of the ideas you were discussing in our last management meeting."

"My retirement, you mean. You can just say it. You won't offend." Sadik laughed.

"Yes, I'm sorry." Esin smiled in return, then became suddenly serious. "I'll be frank with you. I would like to buy your shares in the company before you retire. That'll give us a chance to transition properly and make sure the best interests of the company are served."

Sadik focused in on the woman. All humor disappeared from his expression. He contemplated his words and then spoke. "With the utmost respect for all you've done, I can't do that. This is a family company. One day, when they're old enough, I want my children, Ramiz and Xanthe, to be part of its growth."

Esin nodded, her eyes never leaving the older man. She said nothing for a moment, then nodded. "I understand."

"You know how much I've valued your help all these years, and when the time comes, Ramiz and Xanthe will, too." Sadik leaned forward and touched the woman's elbow, his eyes shining at the mention of his children. "They will grow to appreciate you in the same way I do. Also, you already own a sizable share and will be rewarded for that as the company grows."

Esin nodded again.

"Now, let me try this tea. You can only find it in Antalya, you say? If it's that good, maybe we should send you there on business more often."

Esin smiled as Sadik sipped.

"Thank you for coming to see me, sir," Esin said, showing him to the door a few minutes later. "I'm glad we had this conversation, and I am reassured by what you've said."

"That's good," Sadik said, stepping out into the night. An icy breeze passed across his body. He crossed back towards the car and shuddered, wrapping his jacket more tightly around him. He turned and looked up at Esin, standing at the door. "You know, Esin, this really is a beautiful place. Maybe when I'm retired, I'll get one myself."

"Thank you," Esin said. "Yes, maybe you should. We could be neighbors."

Sadik laughed, then opened the door, waved, and slid into the driver's seat.

The car grumbled and roared into life, headlights cutting a beam through the trees.

The gearbox engaged, and the car crunched across the snow back towards the mountain road.

Esin raised one hand in farewell and slid the other inside her trouser pocket. She touched the empty glass vial, the contents of which had been drunk along with Mr. Sadik's tea.

2

Istanbul, Turkey. Present day.

Sunset in Istanbul. Both in Sultanahmet and across the glittering waters of the Bosporus in Dogancilar, an unseen blanket of dusk was gradually being lowered over the city's daylight chaos. In the markets and bazaars, the screeches of merchants muted in the growing shadows. The ghostly, high-pitched, sacred chant of the muezzin, which moments ago had boomed from the city's countless minarets, sunk back into the unquiet night. The faithful were already where they needed to be. Everyone else? Well, they didn't matter.

For this ancient meeting place, a fiercely defended confluence of the continents, night was coming. But night was not as pure as it once had been. Over the last century, desire and technology had diluted its power. Soon, darkness would spread across the sky, but not through the labyrinthine streets of the city. There, lights would continue blazing as the nocturnal circus bounced and bellowed its way through another turbulent night.

In the district of Samatya, an Ejder Yalcin armored combat vehicle, civilian issue, pulled from an underground parking lot. The giant vehicle's indicator light flashed briefly before the burly machine pulled out onto the road. A slim man on a motorbike raised his hand in protest. Then, upon seeing something through the thick glass windscreen, lowered his fist and allowed the vehicle to pass.

Another identical vehicle followed, then another. Reaching the end of the street, they turned onto the freeway, which skirted the edge of the Bosporus. The water was inky black now, only the milky white scars of propellers indicated anyone was out there at all. On the Asian shore, lights shimmered through the cool evening air.

The three vehicles picked up speed, moving out into the fast lane to overtake a lumbering tanker. A taxi darted from their path, the driver squinting against the dazzling headlights.

Three indicator lights clicked on together. Without breaking their formation, the vehicles moved onto a slip road. Sliding past the tourist sign for Sultanahmet—Istanbul's historic center—the vehicles dropped into higher gears for the climb ahead.

Groups of tourists mingled with the locals, seeking a restaurant or wandering toward the Golden Horn. The nightclubs that occupied the steep streets of Galata prepared for the night ahead. In Istanbul, the night was young.

The vehicles growled and thudded up the incline. Black smoke rose in clouds from their exhaust pipes. Reaching the summit, they turned right towards the impressive towering forms of the Blue Mosque and the long-disputed jewel in Istanbul's crown—the Hagia Sophia.

The vehicles slowed further now.

A group of tourists watched them pass before moving with disinterest to photograph something else.

The vehicles slowed and then crunched to a stop before an iron gate. A chain secured the gate closed and two security cameras assessed the scene. Beyond the gate's vertical spikes, the imposing dome of the Hagia Sophia rose into the sky.

The vehicles waited, unmoving, belting hot gasps of exhaust.

A clang and rattle reverberated from the gate as an unseen hand yanked the chain from its fixings. Slowly, on antiquated hinges, one of the gates swung open. A man crossed through the sharp beams of light. He glanced up at the vehicles, his eyes shining in momentary illumination. He leaned into the other gate, toes curling in the soles of his shoes. Eventually, with an almighty shove, the gate swung open.

A guttural rumble issued from the leading vehicle. A plume of smoke rose from the exhaust as the vehicle pulled inside.

Orange floodlights washed the area in an eerie glow. The vehicles crawled in formation, following the rear wall of the building. Reaching a large door, they pulled to a stop.

The noise of the city swelled around them, the distant sound of idle chatter drifting on the breeze. Lively Turkish folk music wafted from somewhere nearby.

The vehicles' lights remained on. All four doors of the front and rear vehicles swung open. Boots crashed onto ancient stones, worn smooth over centuries by the feet of the faithful, as eight men exited the vehicles. They moved in practiced formation around the central vehicle. It wouldn't be the formation, however, that might interest a passing observer, but the sub-machine gun each man clutched to his chest.

Four men turned their backs to the vehicles and surveyed the surrounding area. The other four moved towards the left passenger door of the central vehicle. The largest of the men stepped forward, extended his gloved hand, and lifted the handle. The locking mechanism clicked and then disengaged. The door swung open.

"Mr. Fasslane," he said, locking eyes with the man inside. "The Hagia Sophia. We are here."

Brent Fasslane stood and pulled a deep breath of the rich Turkish air. He was used to it now. He always thought that it tasted somehow sweeter than his home in New York. He glanced at the sky and thought about the call to prayer he'd heard while they were preparing. Although Fasslane didn't understand the meaning, he liked the sound for some reason.

Somewhere unseen, a siren wailed and then waned. A strong breeze charged in from the direction of the Sea of Marmara, bringing the gentle note of burning incense with it.

"Sir." The man beside him placed a gloved hand on his arm. Like everyone in the organization, his English was impeccable, although accented. Fasslane's eyes moved across the scar, which ran across the man's left cheek. "We must go inside. They're waiting for you."

"Sure," Fasslane said, glancing at a rooftop restaurant across the square. The diners were just discernible through the bars of the fence. "It's a big night. We've waited long enough for this."

3

———

Uludağ, Turkey. Ten years ago.

Ahmet Sadik swung the Alfa Romeo in the direction of Bursa. The sky was black and clear now, the color of the day having drained whilst he was inside.

He fanned his fingers in front of the car's air vent for a few moments. Hot air slipped across his skin, then turned cold. The car's heating system fought a losing battle against the sub-zero temperatures of the mountainside. Over six thousand feet above sea level, it was bound to get a little chilly from time to time.

That was the thing with classic cars, Sadik thought. They weren't as efficient as the new ones. Sadik tapped the walnut dashboard affectionately—regardless of the minor inconveniences, he wouldn't change it for the world.

He powered around the corner and glanced out across the valley. Trees quivered beneath a thick coating of silver frost. The moon hung ripe and low in the sky, as though ready for harvest. Somewhere in the distance, the lights of the town flickered.

There was something beautiful about the mountains, Sadik supposed. They were stark, bleak, unforgiving, almost... what was the word—he ran a hand through his graying beard—*sublime.*

Sadik pictured himself in a cabin like Esin's—cooking on the open fire, walking through the snow. There was something sort of... romantic about it.

Sadik shivered as a strafe of cold air forced its way through the gap around the door. No, this was far too cold. When he retired, Sadik would move to the beach. Turkey had enough beautiful beaches to choose from. Maybe he would even change beaches every so often—just for the heck of it. Sadik leaned back into the seat and felt the imagined warmth of the beach tingle his fingers.

Another bend loomed ahead. A steel barrier flashed past the car's left side, beyond which the snowy mountainside tumbled into unlit valleys. On the right, a rock wall reared upwards. Snow and ice glistened from jutting outcrops. Fingers of frost hung down wherever they were able.

Sadik applied the brake slowly. His feet felt cold. Freezing. Almost as though they weren't there at all.

As the car hurtled towards the impending bend, Sadik's vision began to blur, the edges of his sight darkening like a vignette effect. His head felt heavy as if filled with lead, and a wave of dizziness crashed over him. He blinked hard, trying to clear his vision, but the world around him seemed to tilt and sway. The once-solid lines of the road melted into a swirling mass of white and gray.

Sadik depressed at the brake again. Nothing happened. He glanced down at his legs. Something was off. Strange. Sadik took one hand from the wheel and rubbed it across his knees. There was no sensation there at all. His legs weren't just cold—they had no feeling at all. They were like two blocks of ice. Inhuman. Immovable.

He glanced down. His neck moved an inch and then lolled forward. He tried to straighten up but couldn't. Panic clawed at his chest. He took a labored breath and barely lifted his head.

Sadik's grip on the steering wheel loosened, his fingers growing numb and unresponsive. He tried to focus on the road ahead, but his thoughts were becoming increasingly muddled, a thick fog settling over his mind. The realization that he was losing control hit him like a physical blow. Shock moved up his spine like a bolt of lightning.

He clenched the wheel with all his strength, his last vestige of control. His tendons bulged like tree roots. With all his remaining strength, emitting a desperate hiss of air, Sadik swung the wheel.

With a final, desperate effort, Sadik wrenched the wheel to the right, aiming for the solid rock wall rather than the treacherous chasm that yawned to his left. The car veered sharply, tires screeching against the icy asphalt.

The car struck the rock wall with a sickening crunch. The sound of metal crumpling and glass shattering filled the air. The headlights smashed instantly, plunging the scene into darkness. A discordant symphony of buckling metal followed as the car's frame contorted under the immense force of the collision.

Inside the vehicle, the steering column snapped. The front wheels, no longer under control, twisted at an unnatural angle. The tires skidded across the icy road. Sharp, unforgiving rock pummeled the right side of the car. Internal pipes and wires, unable to withstand the immense pressure, split and ruptured, sending sprays of gas and liquid into the air.

The Alfa, its forward motion not yet spent, spun violently to the left. Bits of metal and plastic, torn from the car's body, scattered in its wake. After a sickening half-turn, the vehicle slammed sideways into the rock face once more. The impact sent shards of glass flying inward, peppering the inside with a hail of razor-sharp fragments.

The passenger door, already weakened by the initial impact, buckled and bent under the onslaught of jagged stone.

As if in slow motion, the battered Alfa rolled a few more feet backward, its tires hissing as they slowly deflated, until finally, the car ground to a stop. Beneath the crumpled hood, the engine ticked softly. A single indicator light, miraculously still functioning, flashed an erratic pattern.

All was quiet. Somewhere in the woodland, an animal called and scurried through the frosty undergrowth.

The sharp lights of another vehicle swept down the mountainside. They lanced out across the valley and then swung in towards the wreck. A deep diesel grumble drifted on the breeze. The vehicle crept around the corner, a Land Rover Defender, and picked its way slowly down the slope. Fixing the Alfa Romeo in its headlights, it slowed. The engine dropped into its lowest register. Gravel and ice snapped beneath the tires. The Land Rover pulled to a stop a few paces from the Alfa Romeo. Sharp ends of twisted metal glinted menacingly in the headlight's glare. The handbrake snapped on, and the passenger door opened.

Esin Kartan strode towards the Alfa Romeo. She wore a large coat now, the fur lining turned up against her neck. She reached the driver's door and peered in. Cocooned in gnarled and warped metal, Sadik stared back at her.

For a moment, it surprised her that his eyes were wide open. Then she remembered that the drug she had given him would just have rendered him immobile. Of course, his eyes would still be open. He would see and hear everything around him—just not able to react.

Esin smiled down at the man who she had worked beneath for almost fifteen years. No more of that. Now it was her time to lead.

"Balik!" she shouted back at the Defender. The driver's door swung open, and a heavy-set man clambered out. The man walked over to the Alfa Romeo. His face was set in a grizzled frown. A scar on the left side of his face shone silver in the moonlight.

"Get this door open." Esin pointed at the Alfa Romeo's twisted door.

The man punched in the remaining glass with a gloved hand, grabbed the frame, and yanked the door open.

Esin crouched beside Sadik. "It's such a shame it had to end this way," she said. "I gave you the opportunity to sell to me, but you couldn't do it, could you?" She signaled for Balik to fetch something from the Land Rover. "You had to give those spoiled brats of yours the chance. Where was my chance, hey? I worked tirelessly for you for fifteen years, and you wanted to pass it all on to someone who's done nothing —just because they're part of your disgusting family."

Balik returned from the Defender and handed Esin a length of plastic tube.

"Don't worry. This will be quick. Also, don't worry about your children. They'll be fine, as long as they're not as stubborn as you."

Esin forced Sadik's mouth open. A gurgling sound came from the old man's mouth, and his eyes bulged in fear. Esin forced the plastic tube down his throat. When the tube was in position, she stood up, holding the other end.

Esin clicked her fingers, and Balik passed her a plastic

funnel. Esin attached the funnel to the end of the tube, then Balik handed her a bottle of vodka.

"Driving on these roads is dangerous at the best of times," Esin said, pouring the contents of the bottle into the funnel. The liquid slid down the tube and into Sadik's stomach. A gurgling sound came from the man's throat.

"To drive on these roads after a drink would be deadly." Esin threw the half-emptied bottle into the car, pulled the tube violently from Sadik's mouth, and walked away from the vehicle.

Balik slammed the driver's door and then crossed to the Land Rover. He removed a cable from the front of the Defender and then hitched it to the back of the Alfa. He climbed into the Land Rover and dragged the Alfa Romeo up the road. Metal screeched against the asphalt, dragging snow and ice with it. Balik revved the engine, positioning the Alfa Romeo in front of a gap in the barrier. A hundred feet below, snow-covered trees shimmered in the moonlight.

Balik stopped the Defender, got out, and unhooked the Alfa Romeo.

Esin watched the scene from the far side of the road, her face distorted into a grin.

Balik climbed back into the Land Rover, revved the engine, and rammed into the Alfa. Metal scraped and screeched. Balik swung the wheel hard to the left, forcing the Alfa from the road.

For a moment, it looked as though the little car was reluctant to go, then it wailed and scratched across the tarmac. Balik pushed the Defender harder. Clouds of fumes streamed from the exhaust.

The Alfa Romeo reached the precipice. Esin stepped closer, enraptured by the scene.

The front wheels hung over the edge. Mud and chunks

of ice and snow rolled and skipped down the slope as though encouraging the car to follow in their wake. Hundreds of feet below, a slither of open water glinted in the soft moonlight.

The Land Rover's engine growled again.

The Alfa Romeo screamed forward, the body now angling downwards. The chassis rocked a few times before coming to rest at an awkward angle.

Balik revved the engine once more, but Esin held up her hand to stop him. She signaled he should pull away.

Balik clicked the Defender into reverse and slid back across the road.

Esin stepped up to the Alfa Romeo. She placed both hands against the remains of the rear bumper and shoved. At first, nothing happened. Then, with a crack and a scrape, the car shifted.

Esin stood back and watched, her arms folded, as the Alfa Romeo slid and spun out of sight.

4

———

Brighton, England. Present day.

Leo knew they intended to kill him. He saw it in their faces, in the way they moved in the shadows. These people, these things, didn't care who you were. They had one thing in mind, and if you were in the way, you were as good as dead.

He raised the gun to his shoulder, the way they had shown him half an hour earlier beneath the brightly lit fluorescents of the *Deployment Zone*. He looked carefully down the barrel. The thing was heavy, cumbersome, and foreign. He moved forward awkwardly, scanning left and then right.

A light in the next room flickered on, exposing bare walls. A *Danger, Deadly Infection* sign hung on one screw. Two yellow oil drums lay on their sides. Smoke seeped through a broken ventilation pipe.

A shriek echoed through the building from somewhere behind him. Ice shot through his veins and his breath caught in his throat. Footsteps pounded against bare floors.

The cry came again, halfway between animal and

human. Something behind him rattled and scurried. Leo's heart hammered against his rib cage.

Leo spun on his heels, failing to keep the gun level with his eyesight, as he'd been told. He saw the creature too late. The thing half ran, half lumbered towards him, bulging eyes glistening and sharp teeth gnashing. In the pulsing red light, Leo saw it had half of its face missing. The jawbone was visible through a missing patch of cheek.

Lights strobed and flickered. A high-pitched, animalistic cry filled the air.

Leo fumbled with the gun, aiming it at the creature. He squeezed off a shot. The gun popped and recoiled. The shot sailed wildly above the creature's head.

The creature growled hungrily as it charged nearer.

Leo's breath caught in his throat. He aimed square at the chest of the monster and pulled the trigger again. The creature howled in pain and reeled back, clutching its chest. Leo shuddered. The creature sunk to its knees, pain burning in its eyes.

A monstrous noise filled the air. But this noise came from behind him. Leo stepped back and spun again. Less than six feet away was another creature. It was similar to the first, except this one had an exposed bone where the left arm should be.

The creature lunged forward, a painful cry issuing from its lips. Leo fumbled with the gun, squeezing the trigger far too late. Two rounds pinged wildly around the room.

The creature cried again, lunged forward, and then bright white light filled the room.

"Game over. Well done, mate. Return to the Deployment Zone." A disembodied voice spoke through hidden loudspeakers.

"Who comes up with this stuff?" Leo asked twenty

minutes later as he and Allissa stepped out into the afternoon air. Leo glanced back at *Living Dead* stenciled above the door of the old industrial building.

"I don't know, but it was great, wasn't it!" Allissa said, glancing down at the sheet of paper detailing both hers and Leo's performance. "You know, you did better than I thought you would. You actually got the first two."

"Thanks, guys," shouted two men, smoking cigarettes by the door.

Leo glanced at them. One had a fake side of his face, showing a protruding jawbone. The other had a prosthetic arm with an exposed bone. The special effects looked much less realistic in the daylight.

Leo smiled and raised a hand, wondering if that would be the weirdest job ever. It was certainly up there, he concluded.

"Hold on a second," Leo said, realizing what Allissa had said as they crossed the road and ambled towards the seafront. "You didn't think I would shoot anything at all, did you?"

"I didn't say that. I just didn't think it played to your finely tuned skill set."

Leo laughed out loud. "I'm versatile, you know. Both brains and brawn!"

It was Allissa's turn to laugh. They turned onto the seafront and crossed onto the promenade. Summer had waned some time ago, taking with it the restless heat that had unsettled the whole of Europe for many weeks.

Leo eyed a man walking on the beach, a long coat drawn tight around him, a dog sniffing at his heels.

"It was good fun, though," Leo said, smiling.

Allissa didn't reply but slotted her arm through his.

The promenade before them was quiet. Brighton had

reverted to its normal, loveable self after the chaos of the summer. In the balmy summer heat, the city became a caricature of a Victorian watercolor or a scene from a Graham Greene novel. Music streamed from open-fronted bars and restaurants. Loud conversation and fits of laughter erupted from large groups of people. Antique merry-go-rounds competed with the clamor of street musicians.

Leo and Allissa strolled in silence for a few minutes, both enjoying the sound of the sea and the sting of the air against their faces. Then, they crossed the road and headed towards their apartment, two streets back from the promenade.

The Victorian building which contained their apartment came into view. At some point during the twentieth century, the building had become three separate residences, and theirs was at the top.

A white van rumbled past them and squealed to a stop outside the building. The vehicle clicked into reverse and pulled into a vacant parking space, two wheels mounting the curb.

Allissa pointed at the van, smiling. "Hey, he's in your space!"

"I know. Maybe he didn't see the reserved sign." After a spate of parking tickets totaling more than the value of the Leo's car, he'd finally sold it.

A man got out of the van, paced around to the back, and swung open the rear doors. He fumbled around for a few seconds, then emerged with a *For Sale* sign. The man approached the front of Leo and Allissa's building, and zip-tied the sign to a gatepost.

Leo and Allissa crossed the road. As they neared, the writing on the sign became clear—*for sale, top-floor apartment*— followed by the name of a local estate agent.

5

Ankara, Turkey. Present Day.

The air crackled with tension as Esin Kartan's high heels clicked against the polished marble floor. The receptionist's voice echoed behind her, "Ms. Kartan, the Minister will see you now."

Esin paused, her steely gaze locking onto the woman behind the imposing wooden desk. With a curt nod, she smoothed down her impeccably tailored trouser suit, a creation from her favorite Venetian tailor.

As she strode towards the Minister's inner sanctum, Esin's mind raced with the gravity of the moment. The fate of Sadik-Tech, and indeed her own legacy, hung in the balance. If she could secure this deal, it would catapult the company to the forefront of Turkey's corporate landscape. Failure, however, was a prospect she refused to entertain.

The nationwide system developed by Sadik-Tech promised to revolutionize the country, registering every citizen on a comprehensive database. It would track criminal behavior, regulate access to public services, and fortify Turkey's borders against those who sought to exploit its resources. More importantly, it would grant Esin an unprecedented level of control over the personal information of 85 million people. In the digital age, data was the new currency, and Esin was determined to become its master.

She crossed the threshold and glanced around at the pompous opulence of the Minister's office. The Turkish flag, its vibrant red fabric engulfing the white crescent, hung limply behind the Minister's desk. Esin saw the symbol for what it had become—a mere decoration in the hands of a self-righteous bureaucrat.

"Thank you for coming to see me, Ms. Kartan," the Minister greeted her, his eyes barely lifting from the papers scattered across his desk. He gestured towards the plush leather chairs, an invitation Esin accepted.

Pleasantries were exchanged, but Esin's patience wore thin. The Minister's nervous tapping against the proposal document betrayed his unease, and Esin's smile grew sharper in response.

"I have discussed your proposal with the president and our security advisory board," the Minister began, his voice wavering. "It's a very well thought out system, which we can see you have tested thoroughly."

Esin leaned forward, her eyes glinting with anticipation. The countless hours and millions of lire poured into the project were about to bear fruit.

"However," the Minister continued, his gaze retreating to the safety of his desk, "the government feels that we are not in a position to move forward with such a proposal at this time. We do not feel such measures are necessary."

The room grew still, the weight of the Minister's words

hanging in the air like a suffocating fog. Esin's face hardened, her eyes burning with barely contained rage.

"With respect, sir," she hissed, her voice dripping with venom, "we are becoming one of the most poorly treated countries on the world stage. This sort of system, as the proposal sets out, would have us controlling our borders, increasing taxation revenue, and leading the way with the fight against crime."

The Minister shrank back, his resolve crumbling under the intensity of Esin's glare. "I'm sorry it's not the news you wanted to hear, but we do not feel such measures are necessary at the moment."

Esin rose to her feet. "That, Minister, is a decision you will live to regret."

With a final, withering look, Esin Kartan turned on her heel and stormed out of the office, her mind already churning with the next steps in her grand plan. If the government wouldn't embrace the future she offered, she would force their hand. One way or another, Sadik-Tech would rise to the top, and Esin would be the one to lead the change.

Esin's fingers tapped an erratic pattern as the elevator lumbered towards the seventh floor. The journey back from Ankara had been frustratingly slow, and she was now late. But she didn't care. The other members of the board—all spineless, idiotic men—would prefer it if she weren't there at all. That wasn't an option. As the Chief Executive Officer and one of Sadik-Tech's major shareholders, Esin wasn't going anywhere. Plus, she was the only one doing anything about their present financial shortfalls.

The elevator slowed, and then, after a series of minor adjustments, the doors strained open. The executive offices on the top floor of their building were quiet. Esin swept through the double doors of the conference suite.

Eight men, dressed in suits of gray or brown, turned to watch as Esin entered the room, their eyes following her every move.

Esin felt their gazes trailing up her trim body, finally meeting her steely eyes. She relished the attention, having long ago learned to use it to her advantage. Her tailored suits were a weapon, designed to command respect and instill a sense of unease in those who dared to underestimate her.

"I trust you have good news for us, Ms. Kartan," the man at the head of the table, Mr. Ersoy, said, his voice tinged with apprehension.

Esin paced dramatically to the window. She stared out at the city below, allowing the silence to build before turning to face the room, fixing Ersoy with one of her infamous hard-eyed stares.

"I'm afraid there has been a setback, Mr. Ersoy," she said, her words cutting through the room like an icy breeze.

Ersoy straightened up in his seat, his discomfort evident as he pushed his glasses further up his nose. Beads of sweat peppered his brow.

A grumble of derision rose from the other men around the table. They shifted uneasily in their seats.

Esin strode across the room and lowered herself into the only vacant chair at the table's far end. She slid a pen from her handbag, the simple action a display of her unwavering control over the situation.

"You led us to believe," Mr. Osman spoke up, his voice quivering slightly, "that you had this under control. In fact, in the revision of the minutes from the last meeting, which you have just missed, you said quite clearly this wouldn't be a problem."

Esin pointed her pen at Osman, her gaze unwavering. "I may have many skills, Mr. Osman, but alas, I cannot predict the future. I'm afraid the Minister is going to need a little more convincing that our product deserves a national rollout."

The men tutted and shook their heads, their disappointment and anger simmering just beneath the surface.

"Did you not make him understand the precarious position Turkey is in?" Ersoy demanded, his voice rising with each word. "They have whipped us from both sides for too long!"

The men grumbled in agreement, their voices overlapping as they aired their grievances.

Esin interrupted the growing chaos with a fist crashing against the table, silencing the room in an instant. "Yes, of course I did. He knows the issues, but he is a weak man. He does not want to stand up and make the difference we do."

"What do you propose?" Osman asked, peering over his glasses, his earlier bravado replaced by something akin to intrigue.

Esin smiled wryly, relishing the opportunity to assert her dominance. "Well, gentlemen, I have a plan. We need to show the Minister how useful our system could be."

The men leaned forward, their eyes wide with a mixture of fear and anticipation.

"We offer them a system that keeps people in line, yes?" Esin looked from one man to the other. Each nodded in turn, their attention now firmly in her hands.

"Then we need people to step out of line. We need some

trouble, some panic, some chaos, and soon the government will be begging for our help."

The men around the table glanced nervously at each other, the weight of Esin's words settling heavily upon their shoulders.

Ersoy spoke up, his voice trembling slightly. "As ever, Ms. Kartan, I am impressed by your nerve and ambition. What if this comes back to bite us?"

Esin stood, her presence commanding the room. "It won't," she said. "But just to be sure, you should take an extended holiday. That way, in the very unlikely event of any problems, you can deny all knowledge."

The men nodded. Their relief was palpable as they clung predictably to the lifeline Esin had thrown them.

"How long will this take?" Osman asked, his voice barely above a whisper.

Esin turned to face the men. She glanced at her fingernails before examining each man in turn.

"Gentlemen, it has already begun."

6

———————

Istanbul, Turkey. Present Day.

Brent Fasslane walked into the belly of the Hagia Sophia, and like everyone else—no matter how important you were —looked around the vast space. Now, with the sun long sunk beyond the Marmara Sea, the windows were dark. Well-positioned spotlights illuminated the room's great architectural and decorative features. The place had, Fasslane reminded himself, been the largest enclosed space on the planet for almost a thousand years. It had been a church, then a mosque, then a museum, and soon was to become a mosque again. Whatever those terms meant, and the religions that they represented, they didn't matter one bit to Brent Fasslane. What he had to say in his upcoming book would shatter millennia of religious scripts, or so he believed.

Fasslane followed his security detail to the center of the vast space's western facade. Now, in the dimness, Fasslane noticed that a temporary wall dissected the huge space. It ran from one column on the left to its opposite on the right and completely obscured the far side of the room. Six feet in height, the wall blocked his view of anyone on the other side but allowed an undisrupted vista of the building's grand roof and walls.

The leader of Fasslane's security detail paused and muttered into his radio. A tinny voice came in reply.

Fasslane listened but couldn't understand a word. Then he noticed another noise rebounding from the ancient stone. Fasslane stood still and listened. He focused on the hushed whispers. Now he could hear it properly, it sounded like hundreds of people whispering nearby.

"They're ready for you," the guard said, pointing towards the wall. His gray eyes bored into Fasslane's. "Remember, fifteen minutes maximum. We do this, and we get out of here. We're already risking too much."

Fasslane nodded, the excited beat of his pulse now rising above the sibilant murmurs.

The guard pulled aside a wide curtain, revealing a brightly lit platform beyond which hundreds of people waited expectantly. The man nodded for Fasslane to pass through, then lifted the radio to his lips. "Everyone at their stations, he's coming out. Remember, fifteen minutes."

"I got you," Fasslane said, stepping towards the stage.

With his hands clenched into fists, Fasslane paced onto the stage. If things tonight went as he and his associates planned, this would be a historical moment. He, and this night, would go down in history.

Fasslane looked out at his audience. Hundreds of people, seated in neat rows, stared back at him, unblinking. Then, Fasslane noticed people crowded in at the back of the space too. Under the ornate arches of the building's main entrance, they bustled for space, elbowing each other out of the way. A camera at the back recorded his every move, as did two cameramen working the stage.

"A moment in history," he repeated to himself.

Fasslane took a deep breath, straightened his jacket, and crossed to the lectern.

No one in the audience moved or spoke.

Fasslane placed his thick knuckles on the lectern and took a deep breath. He was used to people shouting him down, belittling his theories, treating what he said as lies or parody. People rarely sat in stunned silence, waiting for him to speak.

Fasslane liked it. Tonight, he wouldn't disappoint.

Fasslane cleared his throat. Picked up by sensitive microphones on the lectern, the sound rebounded around the space.

He glanced up at the ornate decorations. Giant golden discs, covered with Arabic writing, sparkled in the low light. No one was looking at the building, though. Brent Fasslane was in the spotlight tonight.

"A new world order is coming," Fasslane begun, his voice strong and powerful. Honed on protest marches of the eighties and nineties, he knew how to speak to a crowd. "Most people don't want to see it, they are blind to it, they ignore it. But I speak to you today, as a man whose eyes are well and truly open. Whether you see it yet, whether you want it yet, a new world order is coming." Fasslane let his voice trail off.

He paused and scanned the crowd.

"The governments of this world don't want you to see it. They don't want you to accept it. People like me, who talk about it, are discredited, or even disposed of." Fasslane listed several people who had died under suspicious circumstances. "But change is inevitable. No man can hold back the tides. It is coming, and you will have to decide what to do about it." Fasslane raised a fist.

"I stand here today as an American... A former American," he corrected himself. "When I burned my passport,"—a publicity stunt a few months ago— "I said enough to the rule of people who don't look out for my concerns. They tried to discredit me with bogus accusations of the worst kind. They tried to take away my freedom and belittle what I said. More importantly, though, they tried to pull the wool over your eyes. My ideas are too strong, too dangerous. I have spent my whole life collecting and cataloguing evidence which proves, without doubt, how greedy and self-obsessed our leaders have become. Like the fat pigs on an Orwellian farm, they feast on the spoils of famine, war and sickness, while the rest of us suffer." His face morphed into a solemn expression, and he stared at a point on the back wall.

"They see us as objects from which to take their pound of flesh. To them, you are nothing more than an asset to be used, and used, and used." Fasslane paused for a moment, reading the crowd. Hundreds of serious faces gazed back at him in enraptured silence. A thin smile crept onto Fasslane's lips—they were taking it exactly as he'd hoped. Fasslane took a deep breath and then continued.

"This is the same across the world, not just in my homeland. In Europe, in Australia, in every developed country in the world, you are just a number in a system, you are a digit on a spreadsheet. You are born, you pay your taxes, and you die. The worst thing, no one even sees the bars of the cage they're in. Anyone who questions, who searches for something more, is shunned, burned, discredited, even killed. But no more!" Fasslane's fists crashed down onto the lectern. "It is only because countries like yours, and people like you, who have provided me with safety during this turbulent time, and are able to see through this, that I can even say this at all. If it weren't for you, I would be dead, discredited or imprisoned. Free speech is something we are supposed to value, but only when you're saying what *they* want. That is, until now." Fasslane extended a finger and shook it towards the audience. He checked his watch. He had less than five minutes left.

7

"When I escaped persecution in what is supposedly called the free world"—Fasslane's chubby fingers became quotation marks— "I brought with me all the proof I had collected. My life's work. These documents include records of bribes and profiteering of the worst kind. There are interviews with top politicians and business leaders who decided the truth must be told. Most of those brave men and women are no longer with us. Their deaths were not accidental or surprising. I share all this proof in my new book. Five-hundred pages of irrefutable evidence, verifying the constant and transparent corruption of our governments. I share specific details and specific cases where some of our most trusted men and women have betrayed us for personal gain. I give you evidence of the lives, money and reputations that have been ruined at the hands of this system. This is the system that had me tied to it like a prisoner. Scrabbling around in the dust for... for..." Fasslane faltered. He sucked in a deep breath and calmed himself.

His head of security moved out from the shadows and fixed Fasslane with a slate-eyed stare.

Fasslane cleared his throat again and continued in a slow and even tone. "Many countries have already banned this book. More will follow. But here, in the free country of Turkey, you'll be able to get it on every street corner. It is a testament to your leaders that they've allowed me to speak here today, on the eve of this building, once again becoming a holy place. They understand what the world is becoming, and I thank them for their insight."

Fasslane looked straight down the lens of the camera at the back of the building. "You, watching this at home, before it is removed and banned from social media channels, or joining me here today, you are the last glimmer of hope for this world. We must rise against this oppression. We must stamp out this toxicity in our government like we would an illness—cut out the bad so the rest can flourish. I urge you, find a way to get this book!" He grabbed the book from the lectern and held it aloft. "It's already been banned in several countries. The large retailers will not stock it, but you are creative, inventive, unstoppable people and you will find a way." He flicked open the book and swept through the pages. "Exposed between these pages are decades of secrets and lies, laid bare for you to read. Do not vote again until you have read this. Do not put your money in a bank again," he gasped. "Don't even buy a coffee again until you've read this."

The guard who had warned Fasslane to keep to time looked to his watch and shook his head.

"Time is short, and I must go," Fasslane said, placing the book back on the lectern. "I am already in danger, and I don't want to risk the safety of the good men and women who have made this possible any more than necessary. But before I go, please hear this,"—Fasslane extended his finger towards the camera— "you, learning the secrets in this book, are the last glimmer of promise for this world. It gives me hope that there is a place where freedom can be enjoyed. That, I am happy to risk my life for. Thank you. Together, we can create this new world order!"

The sibilant echoes of Fasslane's final words bounced from the Hagia Sophia's antique arches. Fasslane nodded slowly, swept a hand through his hair, then turned and walked from the stage.

The audience's stunned silence faded, and a rapturous applause began. Cheers, clapping and the clattering of chairs as people climbed to their feet boomed through the vast space.

Fasslane couldn't help but smile. The cameras would still be rolling, too. He had no doubt that the stream would be taken down, but with an army of evangelists like those tonight, it would be reposted moments later.

Fasslane turned and gazed up at the building's magnificent domes and arcs. The gold Arabic script glowed pearlescent beneath spotlights. The whole place had an otherworldly appearance. "What a place to start a revolution," he said to himself.

His security men materialized from the shadows and surrounded him. The leader, his face set in a scowl, led them back towards the building's rear exit. The man led them through an arch and into a passage at the back of the building. The applause dulled to a background murmur. The leader paused and spoke hurriedly into his radio. He stared at Fasslane, unbridled dislike in his eyes.

"We move to the door now," he said, leading them away from the light. Four men surrounded Fasslane in formation and moved slowly, crablike, into the shadows. The leader barked an order and flashlights snapped on. Four fingers of light spread out around them.

The applause dwindled completely, and a tension settled over the group. Military issue boots thumped against the flagstones.

Fasslane peered between the men. His adrenaline drained, and, in its place, a vague disquietude rose.

The leader held up a hand, and the men stopped. The leader's hand reconstituted itself with two fingers pointing forward. The two men at the rear moved out to the sides of the space, sweeping their flashlights rhythmically from floor to ceiling and back again. Then the leader's hand pointed to the left. They moved in formation down a narrower passageway.

Following the men, Fasslane realized he didn't know where they were going. He didn't think they had come in this way, although he hadn't been paying much attention.

The men reached a thick wooden door at the end of the passageway.

The leader turned to face Fasslane. "You know what you need to do." The man holstered his gun and raised a small video camera.

"Make it good," the man hissed. "We only have time for one take."

8

———

Brighton, England. Five days later.

"I've got some great properties to show you today," said the estate agent, a blond-haired woman in her mid-thirties. She drove the car at surprising speed toward Portslade. "It's always a busy time of year for us," she twittered on, raising her voice above the sound of an inert pop song booming from the car's stereo.

"Thanks for arranging this at such short notice," Allissa said from the passenger seat.

"That's no bother at all, don't you worry. We'll get you a place sorted pronto. It'll be smarter than that place you're in now. I can tell you that for nothing."

Leo ignored the twinge of insult that flashed through him. He liked their apartment. He'd been there a long time and felt at home with the discolored walls and threadbare carpet. The apartments they had viewed that morning were stark and bare by comparison.

"This is the third property in this building we've let this month." The agent pulled into a parking lot beneath a modern apartment building. "This one is my favorite. You'll see why."

Leo and Allissa had spent the entire morning visiting various apartments around the city. So far, though, none of the places had inspired them. Leo didn't hold out much hope for this one either.

"You're in for a real treat," the agent said, leading them into an elevator and poking the button for the sixth floor.

Finding the *for sale* sign outside their apartment five days ago had been a shock. When they'd climbed the stairs, they'd found a letter explaining that the landlord had died, and his estate was to be sold. They had one month to find somewhere else to live before prospective buyers would start traipsing through the place. Allissa, not one to sit around, particularly while between cases, got straight to the task at hand.

The agent led them out of the lift and down a brightly lit corridor, twittering all the time about the various benefits of this building.

"It's an eco-efficient A-rated development. You've got basement parking and access to the on-site gym and health suite." She unlocked a door at the end of the corridor and turned to face Leo and Allissa. "Honestly, I've saved the best 'til last. You're going to love it." She smiled and pushed the door open.

Allissa stepped inside, followed by Leo. A wall of glass overlooked the city.

"Now that's a view," Allissa said, stepping towards the window.

The city lay out before them—the Pavilion, the Palace Pier and the spidery remains of the West Pier, all backed by the glinting surface of the sea.

"I know, right?" the agent said. "Let me tell you, it's pretty rare to get a place like this."

Leo wandered around the apartment. It was modern, with faux wooden flooring, bright white walls and those tiny lights that are sunken into the ceiling. Leo tried to imagine his tatty furniture filling the place.

"It's a blank canvas," the woman continued. "Once you've got your pictures on the walls, and your things around, you know?" She didn't pause for a reply. "It'll look like a proper home. It's got a modern kitchen, access to…"

Leo tuned away and paced into the bedroom. The stark decoration and lack of character continued in here. It was a nice place, on paper, but he just couldn't imagine himself and Allissa living here.

"Thank you for your time this morning," Leo said ten minutes later when they were back at street level. "We've got a lot to think about now."

"Of course, of course." The agent shook her head. "Don't hang around, though. Things move quickly around here. Do you need a lift back?" The agent pointed at her car.

"No thanks," Leo and Allissa said in unison. "We've got some stuff to do in town," Leo added. They turned and paced in the direction of the city center.

"What did you think of those places?" Allissa said.

"Well, urrm." Leo exhaled. "They were nice, but they just didn't feel, you know, like home. They were all modern and stark. I'm sure we could make it work, but…"

"I know what you mean," Allissa said. "I'm going to miss our place."

"You like living in Brighton now? You don't want to spend your whole life running around the world anymore?"

They turned down one of the narrow streets. Boutique

clothes shops, modern art galleries, cafes and pubs lined both sides. Brighton was alive, even on a weekday afternoon.

"I wouldn't say that." Alissa grinned. "As a base for our operations it ticks a lot of boxes."

"A base? You call our home a base?" Leo rose to the bait.

Allissa laughed at his frustration. "You know what I mean. Don't do this whole emotionally wounded thing." Allissa led them through a group of people. They reached North Street and turned left towards the seafront. A police van rumbled past, with several stone-faced police officers gazing out.

"What's that?" Leo asked. A noise rose above the grumble of the city. The sound of chanting voices carried on the breeze.

"I'm not sure," Allissa said, hearing it too. "But it's coming from this way."

The police van swung into a side road up ahead, sending a group of pedestrians scattering from its path.

"Hey, whatever is going on, we're not getting involved," Leo said.

"Yeah, of course, but it's exciting to just have a look, right? Is that allowed?"

Leo and Allissa turned into the street and the noise increased further. Home to a couple of swanky restaurants and leading on to the gardens of the Royal Pavilion, this particular street was usually quiet. Not today.

Twenty feet ahead, the police van weaved its way through groups of people, blue lights strobing. At the end of the street, people filled the normally sedate Pavilion Gardens, banners, signs and flags held skyward.

The chanting rose again, reverberating from the surrounding buildings. The voices seemed to merge into one, creating a palpable wave of anger and frustration.

Banners and signs bobbed above the sea of heads, their slogans demanding truth and transparency, some even hinting at the possibility of violence if their demands were not met.

The police van's struggle through the dense crowd seemed to only fuel the protesters' ire. People turned and pounded on the vehicle, bashing it on the sides and windows. The officers who emerged were immediately engulfed by the seething mass of humanity, their shouts for order drowned out by the deafening roar of the crowd.

As Leo and Allissa pushed through, the crowd seemed to swell, spilling out from the Pavilion Gardens and onto the surrounding streets. There was a sense of barely contained rage emanating from the protesters, as if they were a powder keg waiting for a single spark to ignite.

Allissa stopped a young woman, striding towards the center of the melee. "What's going on?"

"Haven't you heard? We want them to stop lying to us. We deserve to know the truth," the woman said, her voice raised above the crowd. "Governments, police, armies, the whole lot are based on lies. We deserve better." She pointed towards the crowd. "This is happening the world over. You won't see it on the news, though. Mainstream media will never spread something like this. They're in on it. This is not a protest, you hear me... this is an uprising." The woman disappeared into the baying crowd, threading herself towards the gardens.

A police siren shrieked from somewhere behind them and another police van bullied its way into the street.

"Alright, we'll go," Allissa said, reading Leo's expression.

They turned and pushed their way out of the intensifying crowd.

Cutting their way toward the seafront, Leo and Allissa

passed countless people with signs and banners tucked under an arm or slung over a shoulder. It looked as though the protest—or uprising, as the young woman had called it —was only just getting started.

Leo and Allissa walked the twenty-minute journey back to their apartment in silence.

"I'm going to miss this place," Leo said, turning the corner and looking up at the building.

For a moment, Leo pictured the years he'd spent padding over the threadbare carpet and patching up the chipped wallpaper. Now, with the idea of living somewhere else in his thoughts, he could only picture the good times. He glanced at Allissa beside him.

"Leo, Allissa!" someone shouted.

Both froze in their tracks.

"You've been quite a challenge to find, I—"

It was a man's voice. Well-spoken and articulate.

"I've been looking all over the city. Don't you ever answer your emails?"

Leo and Allissa swung around to see a man rushing across the road towards them. In his early forties, he had graying hair and wore a suit jacket with chinos. He was sweating and bedraggled.

"My name's Marcus Green," the man said, extending a hand. "I'm a journalist. I'm so glad I've found you. I've got a bit of a situation and really need your help."

9

"My name is Brent Fasslane, and I'm going to die for the secrets I know." The voice boomed from Green's laptop. Leo and Allissa leaned in to get a better view of the video. The recording quality was indistinct and grainy. Figures made emerald by the cameras over exposure, moved through the shadows. Feet shuffled and thudded against hard rock. A light snapped on. The small beam illuminated a man's face. Fasslane stood pale and ghostly, his eyes roaming the darkness as though searching for an unseen pursuer.

"I've known that this was going to happen for a long time. My life has been in danger for many years. Too many people want to silence me. I know too much." Fasslane breathed heavily, his voice wavering.

"But please," he said, looking directly into the camera. "It was only a matter of time for them to get to me, but this is bigger than me. This change, this movement, this revolution, this uprising... it cannot be stopped!"

A shudder moved up Leo's spine at the echoed phrase from the woman at the protest.

"It must not be stopped!" Fasslane continued. "Everything I know will come out, whether or not I'm there to see it. I implore you, if you're watching this, you must seek out the truth. You must find the truth... you must." Fasslane's voice trailed off. Shouting bellowed in the distance.

"They're coming now." Fasslane looked left and right and stepped away from the camera, melting further into the shadow. "They're coming." He looked directly into the lens. "I fear my fight is over, but you must continue this. You must seek out the truth and hold those who have caused so much pain accountable."

The shouting came again, closer this time. Fasslane glanced left and then right. In the weak light from a flashlight, his expression paled further. His lips parted. A series of shouts rang out, and the camera fell to the floor. Feet pounded closer, and then the camera died.

The screen of Green's laptop faded to black.

"That was broadcast live on Brent Fasslane's social media channels two weeks ago. No one has seen him since. At first, we thought it was just a publicity stunt around the publication of his book." Green pulled a thick hardback book from his briefcase and dropped it to the coffee table. "But there's been no sign of him since. You've probably seen this book on the news. Many have been lobbying to get in banned, others think it's the truth. They even debated it in parliament."

Leo picked up the book and flicked through the pages.

"On the night he went missing, Fasslane was giving a speech at the Hagia Sophia in Istanbul—"

"The Hagia Sophia? I heard about that recently in the news," Allissa said.

"Yes, the government has just turned it back into a mosque. Fasslane's speech was one of the last non-religious events to be held there. As far as we understand, he's been staying in Turkey. The Americans have requested several times to have him extradited, but the Turkish Government has consistently refused. Anyway, this video must have come from someone on the inside."

Green tapped another key on the laptop. An image from a security camera filled the screen. Three military vehicles sat nose to tail.

"This is at the rear of the Hagia Sophia." Green pointed at the screen. "Look at the timestamp. Fasslane finished his speech just over five minutes before." Green hit play and on the video a door swung open, and a group of men shuffled out. Shadows concealed their faces. Four of them held guns with the confidence of soldiers, and the fifth looked like a civilian. The military men fanned out in a practiced motion, the silence of the footage exaggerating the efficiency of their movements.

"He's very well protected," Leo said.

"Yes, some kind of private security, we think. No idea who's paying for them. It's unlikely the Turkish army would help him in this way, although they're not confirming or denying anything, officially."

One of the soldiers led the civilian into the central vehicle. The other men swept the area in a practiced sequence before climbing into the trucks themselves. Strong headlights blazed from vehicles. Nothing happened for several seconds, and then the leading vehicle slid away slowly.

In silent slow motion, light flickered from the central vehicle and filled the screen. A roaring fireball engulfed the central vehicle, lighting the entire area like a miniature sun. Searing flames, tinged with vivid oranges and yellows, clawing at the shadows.

The force of the blast shattered windows and sent a shockwave rippling outward. Jagged shards of metal, some still ablaze, scythed through the air like deadly projectiles before clattering to the ground. Black, oily smoke billowed upwards in thick clouds.

The explosion died down, showing the once sturdy military vehicle reduced to a twisted, burning husk. Its armored plates were peeled back like the skin of a ripe fruit, exposing the smoldering innards.

Amid the chaos, shadowy figures darted to and fro, some seeking cover, others rushing bravely towards the inferno in a desperate attempt to help any survivors.

"And that's the last we've seen of Brent Fasslane," Green said, stopping the video and folding his arms. "Or at least, that's what everyone thinks."

10

"It is very convenient that this happens the week before his book's released." Allissa picked up the book and leafed through.

"It's more than convenient," Green said. "Not only has this piece of largely unsubstantiated rubbish sold more copies than all of Dan Brown and JK Rowling's work combined, but people are lapping it up. In the US, here in England, across Europe. Since people got their hands on this book, there's been a sharp increase in civil unrest, and the popularity of fringe groups is soaring. People are taking their money from government backed investments, some are even refusing to pay their tax bills."

"What are you suggesting?" Leo said.

"Listen, I'm not saying the world is perfect. I know there are some corrupt politicians—" Green met Allissa's eye. "Sorry, I —"

"Don't worry," Allissa said. "My dad was a corrupt politician. He isn't any more."

"I know the world's not perfect." Green cleared his throat. "But if this level of mistrust goes on, we're heading for something much worse. Large-scale protests, public services falling apart, the police won't be able to cope, people will have to protect their own property. It'll be ugly."

As though on cue, a police car squealed past. Leo thought of the protest they'd observed not an hour ago.

"Do you think there is any truth in the claims he's making here?" Allissa said, flicking through the book.

"There is some truth in some of the claims, but this isn't the way justice is served," Green said. "I've already got a team of people going through the book to see what we can substantiate. If it stands up, we will be handing all our research over to the authorities—that's how justice is done."

"What can we do?" Allissa asked, placing the book on the coffee table and standing to meet Green's gaze full on.

"Hold on a second," Leo said. "You said, 'that's what everyone thinks.' You know something else, don't you?"

Green's face broke into a smile.

Allissa and Leo shared a glance. For a few moments, no one spoke. The gentle murmur of traffic noise drifted through the thin glass and a seagull shrieked overhead.

"We're not doing this unless you tell us everything you know," Allissa said, folding her arms. "We've had way too many people lying to us recently." Allissa and Leo exchanged glances, both thinking about their most recent case, just a few weeks ago in Riga, Latvia.

"Of course," Green said, rubbing his hands together. "I'm not going to keep anything from you. There are a group of radical journalists in Turkey, based out of Istanbul called, *Gerçeğin Koruyucuları*—the *Guardians of Truth*. They're a mysterious bunch. No one knows who they are, but they make it their business to check claims made by governments and big businesses in the media. I've got a contact there, no name, just an email address. Two days ago, I got a link to this video. It hasn't gone public yet. I think they're waiting until they know more." Green tapped on the laptop and another video started. It was a shot of the same three military vehicles but filmed from directly above.

"It looks like drone footage," Allissa said.

"Yes, that's exactly what I thought." Green pointed at the middle vehicle on the screen. "Watch this very closely."

As in the previous video, the men appeared from the building and fanned out around the yard. Three of them crossed towards the central vehicle and got in.

"Watch now," Green muttered.

Leo and Allissa leaned toward the screen. The vehicle's right-hand door swung closed behind the final man. Then, a couple of seconds later, the opposite door opened. Slowly, the men appeared again on the shadowed side of the vehicle. The camera zoomed in. Two more men emerged and crept to the rear of the vehicle. The leading man spoke into a radio and the vehicles' lights snapped on.

"They're dazzling the camera," Allissa whispered.

The men scurried behind the rear vehicle and out of the shot. The drone footage zoomed out again, but they had dissolved into the shadows of the building.

"That footage was a setup," Leo said as the vehicle on the screen exploded.

"Yep," Green said, stopping the video. "Fasslane wants us to think he's been assassinated, because that reinforces the claims he makes in here." Green picked up the book and brandished it like a weapon. "Of course, my team are working to disprove the information in here, but that could take months. There are over five hundred pages."

"People are already rioting about this. We don't have months." Allissa looked from the book to Leo.

"This isn't a protest, this is an uprising," Leo whispered.

"Where do we even begin?" Allissa said.

"We need to know everything we can about Fasslane," Leo said. "Where did he come from? What took him to Istanbul? All of that."

"I've been watching the guy for years," Green said. "He was always going to be trouble." Green pulled a chair from beneath the dining table and sat facing Leo and Allissa. For the next ten minutes, Green ran through all he knew about Fasslane, from his beginnings as a reporter for a right-wing newspaper in New York, to his fleeing the US and finding safety in Turkey.

Leo was impressed by how succinctly the journalist could express large amounts of information. Allissa took notes.

"Have you any idea of where he could be now?" Leo asked when Green had finished.

"He's been in Istanbul a long time, there's no knowing what contacts he's made. I know where we need to start, though."

"Where?" Allissa asked, exchanging a momentary glance with Leo.

"The Guardians of Truth," Green said. "We need to get to Istanbul and make contact with them. Something tells me this video is just the start."

Leo and Allissa nodded.

"Okay." Leo looked hard at Green. Whilst he liked and respected the man, there was one rule he wasn't breaking again. "But Allissa and I work alone."

11

Istanbul. Present Day.

The sun hung low, its fading light casting a hazy glow over the city as Leo and Allissa's taxi veered into a narrow backstreet. The driver brought the vehicle to an abrupt halt, his outstretched finger jabbing insistently at the windshield. Though his rapid-fire Turkish eluded their comprehension, the message was unmistakable: they had reached their destination.

Leo paid the driver, then they bundled out, grabbed their bags and wandered up the street in search of their apartment. Haphazard four-story buildings flanked the street on both sides. A hotel sat beside a small café, whose chairs and tables spilled out onto the road. Allissa paused to watch a pair of cats darting playfully across the street, their fur glossy and bright.

The flight from London Gatwick had been uneventful. Leo had watched Europe sliding beneath, whilst Allissa snored sweetly. As usual, Leo was now exhausted, and Allissa was full of boundless energy.

"There it is," Allissa declared, signaling a building on the left. She crossed to the door and poked at the intercom. A buzzer sounded from somewhere deep within the building. A voice rose a moment later, followed by the patter of footsteps. The lock clicked, and the door swung open to reveal a woman with a mobile phone clamped to her ear.

"Hi," Allissa said, smiling. "We're staying —"

"No English," the woman barked, beckoning them inside. Without a break in her one-sided conversation on the phone, the woman led them up the stairs.

Since the tiny place Leo arranged for them in Hong Kong, Allissa had taken charge of arranging their accommodation. Climbing the dingy staircase, Allissa wondered whether she should have opted for one of the city's large chain hotels. She turned around and caught Leo's eye.

On the third floor, still without a break in her monologue, the woman pointed at a door at the end of the hall.

Leo and Allissa stepped over a mop and bucket and shuffled towards the door.

Leo pushed through the door and into the apartment that was to be their home for the next few days. Leo dropped his bag on the bed and looked around. The place was a simple one-room studio, with a double bed and a compact kitchenette. A door led through to the bathroom, and the other onto a small terrace.

"Not bad," Leo said, glancing at Allissa.

The woman's voice faded as she paced back down the stairs.

"I thought you'd approve," Allissa said, pulling off her shoes. "It was a bargain."

Leo strode to the far end of the room and swung open a glass door.

"Balcony, nice!" He said, stepping outside.

The terrace looked out across the disordered rooftops of downtown Istanbul. Block concrete buildings jostled for space beside the slender minarets and domes. Rusting antennas bristled upwards amid webs of tangled wire and washing flapped from lines.

Allissa stepped out onto the terrace too, squinting in the sunlight.

"Cool place..." The call to prayer boomed from the mosque at the end of the street.

"Afternoon prayers," Leo said with a grin. "How many times a day do you think they'll do that?" he asked.

"Five," Allissa said, returning his smile. "At least."

Allissa peered up at the muscular outline of the Hagia Sophia, just visible up the hill. The ancient edifice dominated the skyline, its massive, bulbous dome and slender minarets etched boldly against the heavens.

"That's our first stop," Leo said, pointing up at the building. "Let's see where Brent Fasslane was last seen alive."

Half an hour later, Leo and Allissa joined the line, which shuffled towards the security checkpoint at the front of the Hagia Sophia.

"I don't think we'll find anything here," Allissa said, peering up at the structure.

"Alright, but it's a place to start," Leo said, shuffling forward. "Getting the feeling of the place is important."

Allissa pivoted on her heel, her gaze sweeping across the expansive square that stretched out behind them. The bustling heart of Istanbul's tourist district, the square, was a vibrant kaleidoscope of activity in the early afternoon light. Throngs of visitors meandered through the open space, clutching maps and cameras.

A constant hum of chatter filled the air, punctuated by

the occasional shout of a tout or the melodic call of a hawker peddling their wares.

To the left of the lively melee, the Blue Mosque's elegant minarets soared skyward. The mosque's intricate tile work glimmered in the sunlight.

On the opposite side of the square, the Obelisk of Theodosius cast a long shadow across the pavement.

The distant clang of a tram rounding a nearby corner snapped Allissa out of her reverie. As the tram vanished behind a wall, Allissa's gaze locked with that of a man standing at the corner. Clad in blue jeans and a black jacket, he stood motionless. For a fleeting moment, their eyes remained fixed on one another. Then, as abruptly as he had glanced in Allissa's direction, the man broke eye contact and melted into the crowd.

"Come on," Leo said, pulling Allissa through the gates and into the security checkpoint.

They stepped into the cool interior of the Hagia Sophia. They paced down a wide stone corridor leading deeper into the building. Allissa gazed up at the walls, painted with frescos of red and cold. She stopped to examine a painting, imagining what story it told.

They shuffled on through another set of doors and into a larger room. This one had a high arched ceiling. Light streamed in thick bars from small high windows.

Allissa and Leo stepped on into the building's central chamber, their necks craning to take in the enormity of the place. The dome, glowing in gold and bronze, shimmered far above them. Great discs adorned with Arabic script hung around the walls.

"Wow! Crazy, isn't it?" Leo whispered in Allissa's ear.

Leo and Allissa walked across the giant room, their feet

sinking into the carpet. Lights hung on long chains, illuminating the stone in a soft, golden glow.

Reaching the far end of the building, Leo dug out his phone. He scrolled through the recording of Brent Fasslane's speech. He looked from the screen to the surrounding building, trying to figure out the layout of the room.

"It looks like the stage was there." Leo pointed to an area in the center.

Allissa glanced at Leo's phone. "Go back to the start. Where did Fasslane enter and leave?"

Leo scrolled back through the video. "You can't see clearly because of that curtain, but I suspect it was there," he said, pointing to an arch in the back corner.

Allissa led them across the room. The arch led into a shadowy passageway, sectioned off by a rope. Allissa paused at the rope and peered into the gloom.

"That must lead out to the back of the building, where we saw Fasslane leave," Leo said.

Allissa nodded, then turned and glanced around the chamber. She froze. Standing on the far side, gazing disinterestedly at a wall, was the man she'd locked eyes with outside. The same slight frame, black jacket, blue jeans.

"That man, over by that pillar," Allissa said, glancing quickly across the room. "He was watching us outside, I'm sure of it. He caught my eye in the line."

Leo feigned a look around the space. "Do you think he's following us?"

"Maybe. He's clearly interested in what we're doing."

The man's stance shifted. He strolled nonchalantly across the room and looked up at the opposite wall.

"Let's give him something to be interested in," Allissa said, stepping over the rope and slipping into the passageway.

Leo cast a furtive glance over his shoulder. The Hagia Sophia's grand chamber lay a mere forty feet behind them, its vast dome commanding the attention of the visitors who milled about, their necks craned upwards and eyes wide with wonder.

As Allissa led them deeper into the off-limits area, Leo pictured the armed guards stationed at the entrance. He felt a growing sense of dread that he and Allissa were heading somewhere they shouldn't be.

Ahead, the passage curved to the left. The dim light from the main room faded and only a faint glow remained to guide their way.

Twenty feet further, a solitary light hung from the ceiling. The light cast an eerie glow upon the rough-hewn stone. The light illuminated a thick wooden door, its weathered surface bearing the scars of countless years.

Leo and Allissa exchanged a glance. Allissa reached out and tried the handle.

Certain it would be locked, forcing them to retreat towards the main chamber, Leo felt the rising sting of anxiety.

Allissa tugged on the door. With a screech of decrepit hinges, it swung open.

Daylight flooded the passageway. Allissa slipped through, with Leo a step behind. They were standing in a secluded courtyard at the rear of the Hagia Sophia. The eerie stillness hung about the courtyard, only broken by the murmur of the city beyond.

"This is where the explosion happened," Allissa said, pacing to the center of the courtyard. "There's the camera." She pointed up at a camera mounted high on the wall.

Leo was about to reply when a sound shattered the

silence. The booming echo of boots on stone floors drifted from the open door.

"Quickly," Leo said, charging back to the heavy door and shoving it. "Someone's coming. Help me push this closed."

Allissa joined him and together they threw their weight against the wood. The door groaned in protest as it swung shut with painful lethargy. The sound of the pursuing foot-steps faded to a dull patter.

"I can't believe you made us do that," Leo hissed, racing toward a gate which he hoped would lead them back onto the street. "The guy in there was probably just a tourist. For once, you're the one who's seeing things."

Allissa didn't respond, her attention fixed on the singed branches of an over hanging tree.

The raised voices from behind the closed door grew louder, the sound of their pursuers drawing ever closer.

"We need to get out of here," Leo said, reaching the gate. His palms slick with sweat, he struggled to release the mechanism. With a final, desperate tug, the gate swung open.

Leo and Allissa stepped through the gate and merged into a crowd of unsuspecting tourists. Leo glanced back as a pair of armed security guards burst out into the courtyard. Leo dipped his head, seized Allissa by the hand and pulled her through the crowd and away from the Hagia Sophia.

"I didn't mean to put us in danger," Allissa said when they were a safe distance away. "I just... I had a feeling about that man, and I couldn't let it go."

Leo slowed his pace and eyed his partner. "You've got to trust your instincts. Do you think you'd recognize him again?"

"I think so," Allissa said, her brow furrowing. "It might be nothing, but—"

"Oh right, so now you say it might be nothing... after you've had us running away from armed guards through the restricted areas of an ancient monument."

"I don't know," Allissa said, her voice trailing off. "He just caught my eye. It was strange. It wasn't like a casual stare. He was watching us."

"We'll keep an eye out," Leo reassured. "Whoever it was, we've lost him for now."

Fifteen minutes later, they climbed the stairs to their apartment. As Leo crossed the threshold into the small kitchen, he froze, ice running through his veins.

"Look at that," Leo gasped, his voice barely above a strangled whisper. He pointed at a note on the kitchen counter. The sight seemed to swim before his eyes.

Allissa rushed to his side, her breath catching in her throat as she read the spidery handwriting alongside him.

Ali's Fish Stall, Grand Bazaar, 3pm tomorrow.

12

———

Balik's knuckles rapped sharply against the door, the sound echoing through the empty hallway. The small brass sign— E. Kartan CEO—vibrated with each knock. He glanced over his shoulder. The other members of the executive team had been conspicuously absent for weeks now. Working from home, they called it. Balik scoffed at the thought. That bunch of layabouts wouldn't know work if it slapped them in the face.

"Come in," Esin's voice rang out, muffled by the door.

Balik turned the handle and stepped inside, the door clicking shut behind him. The spacious office was bathed in bright midday light, the floor-to-ceiling windows offering a stunning view of the city below. Esin sat behind her desk, her eyes locked on the computer screen. In the distance, the Golden Horn glittered like a ribbon of molten gold, winding its way through the jumbled tapestry of Istanbul's buildings.

As Balik approached the desk, the first haunting notes of the Dhuhr—the midday call to prayer—drifted through the open window. Soon, the melody would be echoed by dozens of other mosques, the collective voices of the muezzins cascading over the city.

"We may have a problem," Balik said.

Esin looked up, her eyebrow arched in a silent question. "Oh?"

"Yes, it's the Gerçeğin Koruyucuları."

"The Guardians of Truth," Esin spat, her lip curling in contempt.

Balik nodded. "We've been watching them, as you instructed. They've made a few small claims, but nothing that anyone's paid much attention to."

"Nothing to worry about, then," Esin said, leaning back in her chair, her fingers steepled.

"Well," Balik hesitated, his brow furrowed. "They have made contact, through a journalist who is loyal to their cause, with some investigators from England. I've looked into them, a small outfit who go by the names of Leo Keane and Allissa Stockwell. They've got quite a form for this sort of thing. Remember the scandal with the Latvian government a few months ago…"

Esin did indeed remember the headlines that had dominated the news cycle for a week or so. Half the government, including the favorite to be the next president, had been forced to resign when secret documents were brought to light.

"They arrived in Istanbul yesterday," Balik said, gravely.

"Do you know where they are?" Esin said, her pupils constricting like a predator with sights on its next meal.

"Yes," Balik said, a sly grin spreading across his face. "And I know how to get rid of them."

"I'm listening," Esin said, leaning across the desk.

Balik strode to the door and beckoned in three men inside.

Esin eyed each of the new arrivals in turn. The men were clearly tough and wore the uniforms of the Turkish National Police.

"Gentlemen, you look fantastic," Esin said, a smile playing at the corners of her lips. "Looking at you is enough to encourage anyone to stay out of your way. Very convincing."

Balik pulled a black cap over his head and shrugged on a jacket emblazoned with the national police crest.

"Is everything else in order?" Esin asked. "You have the transport and something to make sure they don't bother us again?"

Balik nodded, his expression resolute. "Yes, everything is in order."

Esin rose from her chair and crossed the room, her hand coming to rest on Balik's shoulder. She looked him in the eye, her gaze unwavering. "Excellent. Get down there and get rid of them."

LEO WATCHED a couple in the window of a café sip at their coffees while poking at their phones. The pair had exchanged less than a dozen words in the time Leo and Allissa had been there.

Leo sighed and glanced at the time—it was a quarter to three. He removed the note which they'd found in their apartment and smoothed it out on the table.

Somewhere behind the counter, a dishwasher chugged, and a radio played tinny pop music. The barista swatted at a fly with a discolored dishtowel.

"What're you worried about?" Allissa asked, watching him from above the rim of her second drink.

"They knew where we were staying." Leo rubbed his hands together and willed away the familiar claws of anxiety. It was a feeling he knew well now, one that he claimed to control but was never totally sure.

"I've no idea how they knew that..." Allissa said, trailing off.

Leo rubbed his hands together again, the tendons in his wrists and forearms bulging.

"It's time to go, anyway," she said, glancing up at the clock on the wall. "We need to find Ali's Fish Stall by three."

Leo nodded, cleared his throat, and stood.

They clattered through the door of the café and into the bright afternoon sunlight. The entrance to the Grand Bazaar sat across a small square. Gold letters in both Arabic and English glimmered from a red archway. The noises of traffic jibed with bubbling conversation.

"Don't you think we should have some kind of back-up plan?" Leo asked, his eyes franticly roaming the square.

A large woman in a bright blue headscarf pushed a trolly stacked with boxes towards the main entrance. A man, thick forearms straining under the weight of two carrier bags, struggled toward a bus stop.

"Like what?" Allissa said. She glanced up at Leo and then slid her arm through his. "Honestly, it'll be fine. It's the middle of the day in one of the city's busiest places. There are security guards, cameras, all that sort of thing."

"Hardly the most dynamic security force," Leo said, pointing at a man in a security uniform smoking beside the entrance.

"It'll be fine," Allissa said, leading Leo inside the Bazaar. The pair were immediately engulfed by a kaleidoscope of colors, sounds, and scents. The ornate tiles that adorned the vaulted ceiling above them shimmered under the bright lights, their intricate patterns of blue, yellow, and mauve creating a mesmerizing tapestry.

Raised voices of merchants and customers boomed through the space, each engaged in a frenzied dance of negotiation and persuasion. The wares of the sellers, displayed in vibrant arrays of color and texture, lined the narrow passageways.

"We've got ten minutes," Allissa said. "We're going to need some help."

"You need a shawl, beautiful fabrics, just try," a young woman shouted from the stall as they passed.

"No," Allissa said, turning abruptly. "But we do need help finding Ali's Fish Stall."

The woman motioned for Leo and Allissa to follow, turned on her heels and charged with surprising speed through the market.

They turned a corner and rushed past rows of beautiful pottery—Allissa craned her neck, glimpsing ornately painted patterns of blue and gold. They reached another junction. Two more market halls spanned out to the right and left.

"That way," Leo shouted, spying the lady in the red shall. Leo swung around a corner, with Allissa on his heels.

The woman with the red shawl was just ten feet ahead now. Leo glanced at the stalls, which in this section of the bazaar sold pots, pans and other home wares.

The woman in the shawl turned right. Cold air moved swept through the bazaar. Leo and Allissa rushed past large displays of meat. Half carcasses lay on slabs of wood. Burley men in blood-stained aprons arranged cuts of meat on beds of ice.

Leo almost lost sight of the woman, then noticed a flash of red turning the corner ahead.

They powered on, narrowly avoiding a man carrying several plucked chickens by the feet. Leo turned the corner and stopped suddenly. Allissa almost ran into the back of him. The woman stood in front of them, smiling broadly. "Ali's is there," she said, pointing to one of the dozen or more fish stalls. "You can't miss him. Man with the beard." The woman's hands cupped her chin to indicate the beard.

"Thank you," Allissa said, rummaging through her pockets. "Let me give you something—"

"No need," the woman interrupted, placing her hand on Allissa's arm. She turned and disappeared, sashaying back through the hordes of people.

"We've got two minutes," Allissa said, checking the time.

The pair rushed up the hall, looking for a man with a beard. Sure enough, three stalls up on the right side, a fishmonger with a giant beard dexterously gutted a fish.

Leo and Allissa stepped forward, out of the flow of people. Leo glanced around. The sounds of negotiation and tapping feet pattered from the ceiling tiles. The shrill ringing of a phone pierced the hubbub. They both ignored the noise, not recognizing the ring tone.

"I guess we wait," Leo said, answering Allissa's unasked question.

The shrill ringing of the phone continued. It was coming from somewhere nearby. People flowed up and down the hall.

"Hey," came a thick accented voice. "You not going to answer that?"

Leo and Allissa looked up, almost in surprise. The bearded fishmonger pointed at the counter beside Leo and Allissa with a blood-stained knife. Leo and Allissa glanced down. A cell phone glowed, ringing noisily.

13

The phone was a basic, low-tech model—a burner. A long and mysterious number scrolled across the display.

The volume of the market rose. Two women, swinging string bags and talking loudly, pushed past. The knife of the butcher, two stalls up, thudded into the chopping block, cracking bones and slicing flesh.

The phone trilled again. It was the sort of noise modern phones don't have. A bleeping electronic howl, never found in the natural world.

"Answer it," the fishmonger growled, his voice low and menacing. He scowled at Leo, his knife poised mid-slice above the body of a great silver fish, its entrails spilling onto the blood-stained counter.

With a trembling hand, Leo snatched up the phone. He scanned the surrounding crowd for any sign of danger.

The phone trilled once more. Leo pressed the button and raised the phone to his ear, locking eyes with Allissa.

"You must listen to me very carefully." A man's voice came down the line, his accent thick and unfamiliar. "I have information that you need to hear, but we don't have much time."

Leo's grip on the phone tightened. He strained to focus on the man's words over the din of the market. Allissa leaned in closer, her brow furrowed in concentration.

"You are in great danger," the caller said.

Before Leo could respond, a burst of noise echoed from the vaulted ceiling. The sound of running feet reverberated from the far end of the hall.

"There are people coming for you. I can get you out of there, but you must do exactly as I say," the caller said, his voice cutting through the rising din.

"Wait, what?" Leo said, his mind racing as he spun toward the noise. "Who's coming for us? Why are—"

Allissa tensed. Her body coiled like a spring as she prepared to run. Her eyes darted from stall to stall, searching for any sign of escape.

"Ninety seconds ago, a group of men entered the Grand Bazaar by the north gate," the caller said. "They are dressed as National Police, but they are not the police. In twenty seconds, they will turn the corner and head your way."

Another cry reverberated through the market. Someone shrieked, followed by the sound of shattering pottery. The roar of thundering boots was clearly audible now.

"Listen," Leo said. "I don't know who you are, or what's going on, but—" he paused, catching sight of Allissa. She stared wide eyed towards the incoming noise. The sound of each boot was distinct now. People shouted as they leaped out of the way. Leo removed the phone from his ear and listened.

"Okay." Leo grasped Allissa's arm with his free hand. "We're listening."

"Turn right and run as fast as you can to the end of the hall," the caller explained. "Then, left at the junction."

Leo grasped Allissa's arm and yanked them to the right. They darted past a family gathered around a fish stall. Leo let go of Allissa's arm and the pair separated to avoid an old man with a walking stick, then vaulted a crate of ice and sprinted for the end of the hall.

"Turn left," Leo shouted, powering around the corner.

Allissa followed a moment later.

The narrow corridor stretched out before them. Storage boxes and trolleys sat piled against the walls.

Leo and Allissa charged down the corridor. The harsh fluorescent glow of the market morphed into bright afternoon sunlight spilling through an open doorway ahead.

"Good, you're doing well," the man said. "Once you're outside, you need to—"

"No, wait," Leo shouted breathlessly.

"What?"

"The gate," Leo panted. "Someone's closing the gate."

Up ahead, a silhouetted figure pulled a metal gate across the entrance. The gate swung across the opening and then clanged shut. The figure engaged a lock, then turned and hurried away.

Leo and Allissa charged on. They sprinted past a stack of boxes and skirted a crate of watermelons left in the center of the hallway. They reached the bars, panting. They were just a few seconds too late, but the figure had already ducked into a crowd.

Allissa pushed the gate as hard as she could. The bars shook but didn't open.

Thumping feet echoed up the passage behind them. A deep male voice shouted commands.

"It's locked," Leo said. "What now?"

"One moment!" The sound of a keyboard rattling came down the line.

"Stop where you are!" A voice reverberated up the passage from behind them. The footsteps stopped.

Leo and Allissa turned slowly. Three men stood at the end of the corridor, each of them muscular and imposing.

"There is no point running. We have you surrounded," one of the men, clearly the leader, said.

Leo kept the phone clamped to his ear.

The men took a step forward. The normal babble of the market drifted down the hallway.

Leo spun around again and glanced through the locked bars of the gate behind them. People meandered in the sunshine down towards the Golden Horn.

"Okay, I've got it. It's a tricky one, but I can still get you out," the caller said, sounding even more urgent now.

"I'm listening," Leo said, breathing deeply.

"Put the phone down," the muscular man barked. He paced down the corridor toward them, reaching for the gun holstered at his hip.

Dressed as National Police—Leo remembered the caller's description—no one would question these men carrying arms.

"There's a door on your right, ten feet away," the caller said. "It shouldn't be locked. Move now!"

14

Leo glanced at the door and then looked back at the men. He hadn't noticed the door on the way past. Painted the same color as the wall, it was easy to miss.

The muscular man's grin widened. His hand hovered above his hip.

"These men have guns," Leo hissed into the phone.

"Don't worry, they won't risk shooting in a public place," the caller replied.

"I'm not so sure," Leo replied, watching the thug's hand move closer to his hip.

"Just trust me," the caller spoke confidently. "Go through that door and you'll see a staircase to your left. Wait for my signal, okay?"

"I'm losing patience now," the thug howled, his voice echoing menacingly. "Put the phone down and step this way." His eyes blazed with a dangerous intensity.

"Just a few more seconds," the man hissed down the phone line, his voice tight with urgency.

Leo leaned closer to Allissa, whispering the crucial instructions. She nodded, her face pale but resolute.

"No one needs to get hurt," the thug sneered. His scarred face twisted into an ugly mask.

An almighty crash boomed from the hall behind the men. Like a cannon shot in the enclosed space, the sound reverberated several times throughout the market. A flurry of cries and shrieks followed. The thugs turned momentarily toward the noise.

"Go, now!" the caller shouted.

Leo leaped towards the door, his feet sliding across the tiles. He covered the distance in three paces and crashed through. The door swung open and slammed against the wall behind, sending a cloud of dust into the air. Allissa followed him a moment later.

The shouts of surprise died away, replaced by the rising voices of the men outside.

Leo glanced around the space, his eyes quickly adjusting to the dim light. A big, industrial freezer sat against one wall. Cobweb-covered crates languished against the other.

Allissa slammed the door shut and pressed her back against it.

"Up the stairs to your left," the caller said.

Leo spun around and saw a narrow staircase leading up behind the row of boxes.

"This way." Leo indicated the stairs.

"No, wait, help me with this." Allissa darted over to the freezer. She shoved it as hard as she could, but the appliance barely moved.

Leo jumped forward to help, and together they heaved the freezer over and shoved it against the door.

The handle twisted, and the door opened an inch before smashing into the freezer.

One of the thugs shoved the door with his shoulder. Frustrated voices streamed through the gap.

"Come on," Leo shouted, pulling Allissa towards the staircase. "That won't hold them for long."

Another shoulder smashed into the door behind them, splitting the wood in two and ripping the hinges from the mountings.

Leo and Allissa charged up the staircase, through another door, and into a narrow passageway. Leo peered through one of several small arches cut into the wall. Several feet below, normal service had resumed in the market hall. People milled about the stalls, and merchants touted for business.

"You'll find a staircase one hundred feet ahead," the caller said. "You need to climb it."

Leo relayed the instructions to Allissa, shouting above the noise of the market.

"How does he know this?" she shouted back.

"No idea." Leo's trainers slid to a stop, sending a cloud of dust into the air.

"I can't see a staircase," he barked into the phone.

Light streamed in thick bars through high windows, illuminating dust swirling through the air.

The noise of a tapping keyboard came down the phone line. "It's there. On the right," the caller replied.

"There," Allissa said, pointing up at the wall.

Leo turned around and looked again. As his eyes adjusted to the light, he saw a thin spiral staircase extending vertically from behind a pile of boxes. A layer of crusted dust rendered it barely visible against the stone.

Leo pulled the boxes aside and grabbed a rung. He shook the structure. The metal clanged and wobbled. He peered tentatively upwards. Thirty feet above, the staircase disappeared into the ceiling.

A crash echoed up the corridor, followed by the raised voices of the men.

"The men have passed the door," the caller said. "You must climb the staircase."

"Up we go," Leo said, thudding up the first two steps. The metal clunked and groaned under his feet. The staircase wobbled, leaning away from the supporting wall. Leo glanced down to and saw Allissa climbing a few steps behind him.

Leo climbed as quickly as he could around the tight spiral. He paused and glanced back down at the floor beneath them. The wobbling was even more pronounced at this height, the whole staircase moving this way and that. Not looking where he was going, Leo slipped on the thin tread. His knee struck the rung and white-hot pain pounded through his leg. The staircase swayed further away from the supporting wall.

Leo grasped the phone tighter to stop it slipping from his hand. He glanced down at the ground between the treads, then instantly regretted it.

The voices of the pursuing men drew closer.

Leo struggled back onto his feet and slowly, painstakingly, continued to climb. Several steps later, he passed the level of the ceiling. Dust coated the rungs even more thickly here. With each step a great cloud of it billowed into the air. Walls of brick enclosed the staircase on all sides.

Allissa crouched and glanced down into the space behind them. The men emerged from the doorway below and ran along the passage, their raised voices filling the room.

Leo forced himself up the final few stairs, every instinct wanting to give up and return to solid ground. He came to a horizontal hatch blocking their passage. He pushed his shoulder into it. The hatch shuddered but didn't move.

"What now?" Leo hissed into the phone.

"That hatch hasn't been opened in over a decade. A strong shoulder should do it," said the caller, as though it were the most obvious thing in the world.

Leo barged it again. The man was right.

"But wait," the man hissed urgently.

"Why—"

"The men," Allissa interrupted. "They haven't realized we're here."

15

———

Leo froze, listening to gruff voices drift from below.

"Wait," the caller said. "They'll pass in a minute."

Leo inhaled, but the breath only partly entered his chest before his anxiety forced it away. He tried again. A snatch of air slipped into his lungs.

"I think they've passed," Allissa whispered. "Leo." She tapped him on the leg.

Leo turned, twisted into the staircase, and looked at Allissa. He took a breath. A nourishing lungful of air filled his chest.

"Go now. Quietly as you can," the caller said.

Leo turned to face the hatch and passed the phone to Allissa. He climbed and pressed his shoulder against the hatch.

"Now," Allissa said, repeating the caller's instructions.

Leo pulled back and then slammed his shoulder into the wood. The staircase clanged, and the wood splintered.

"Again," Allissa hissed.

Leo repeated the motion. The hatch moved an inch but refused to yield. Leo crouched low; his muscles coiled like a spring ready to unleash. He gripped the spine of the staircase, his knuckles turning white, and dug his feet into the rungs.

With a mighty exhale, Leo slammed his shoulder into the hatch. The wood screeched, splintered and then shattered. The hatch exploded outward, its remnants flying out onto the rooftop in a shower of jagged splinters and twisted metal.

The force of the impact sent Leo lurching forward, his grip on the staircase wrenched away by the sudden, violent motion. He scrambled desperately for a handhold, grasping at anything that might arrest his fall.

Allissa lunged forward with her free hands outstretched. Even her lightning-fast response was not enough to prevent the inevitable.

Leo's body slammed into Allissa with the force of a runaway train, sending her reeling backward. Allissa dropped the phone, which went clattering down the stairs. She tried to grip on to the narrow rungs, but the stairs slipped beneath her feet.

With a final, desperate lunge, Allissa's hand closed around a rung. She pulled with all her might, dragging herself and Leo to a precarious stop.

For a moment, they hung suspended between the rooftop and the stairwell. Then, with a shuddering gasp, Allissa pulled them upright.

Leo rested on his elbows for a moment, not daring to look down at the floor, a deadly distance below.

Allissa scrambled out and stood beside Leo on a lower section of the bazaar's roof. The serpentine curves of the tiled roofs stretched out before them. In the distance, domes and minarets pierced the skyline. To the left, another staircase led up onto the great curving roof of the bazaar.

"What now?" Leo said.

"I don't know," Allissa replied. "The phone. It's down there."

Leo looked from the skyline to Allissa, and then back down the hatch.

"We need that phone," Allissa said. "We've no idea which way to go without it."

Leo nodded. "I'll go back."

"No." Allissa grabbed his arm. "I dropped it, I'll go."

BALIK LED his men up the small staircase and into another, larger room. He glanced through a small window in the left wall. The market's hubbub continued below. Satisfied that the window was too small to climb through, not to mention the twenty-foot drop into the market hall on the other side, he ran on.

Balik slowed to pick his way past an overflowing pile of detritus. Ahead, the passage turned to the right. There was no way of knowing how many hidden rooms and passages this building contained.

Balik reached the bend in the passage and paused. The man following close behind him almost ran him over. A narrow opening led off to the left. The floor and the piles of boxes were covered in a thick layer of dust and grime. Balik examined the boxes closely. It was difficult to make anything out in the gloom. He pulled a flashlight from his pocket and clicked it on. He swept the beam across the dust covered boxes but couldn't see any sign that they'd been moved recently.

"They're in here somewhere," Balik said, turning to face his men.

At that moment, he noticed something. The girl scurried down a narrow staircase above their heads. She grabbed something and then rushed back up onto the roof.

"There!" Balik said, pointing toward the woman.

The men swung around and charged toward the staircase.

"Wait a second," Balik said, stopping the pair. "You go up there. I'm going to cut them off outside."

The men nodded and set off up the staircase.

16

Allissa leaped from the hatch, the phone held high. Leo took the phone from her and held it against his ear.

"There you are," said the caller as though this were a perfectly normal encounter. "Now, take that staircase behind you."

"No, wait," Leo said, frustration boiling over. "We've outrun those men. Now tell us who you are and how you know what's going on."

"Look up."

Leo squinted against the sun. He couldn't see anything at first, then slowly, a tiny shape came into view. He heard the soft hum of electric motors. A drone hovered twenty feet above the roof.

"I also have access to the security cameras inside. As for who I am, I'll explain that when we meet."

"When will that be?" Leo demanded.

"Soon," the man said. "But right now, you're going to have to run again. The men have seen you and are climbing the staircase."

The clang of footsteps on the rungs drifted from the hatch. Allissa peered back down into the market.

"They're coming." She looked up at Leo. "What now?"

"That way," Leo said, turning and charging up the staircase. The structure was nothing more than a series of rungs bolted to the bazaar's ancient tiles. At the summit, a row of boards ran in both directions.

Leo reached the top and glanced from right to left. The city spanned out before him like an oil painting. The curving roof of the market rose and fell in great swathes of tile and tin. The domes and minarets of the city's countless mosques punctuated the horizon, and in the distance the stretch of water—the Bosporus—at which Europe stops and Asia begins, shone like a bed of diamonds in the afternoon sun. The only thing to suggest this was not an antique oil painting were the satellite dishes and air conditioning units, which hummed and ticked in the afternoon breeze.

"Turn right," the caller said. Leo glanced above him. He couldn't see the drone against the bright sky. He stepped tentatively from the steps and onto the boards.

Allissa reached the apex and stood beside him. "Where now?"

Leo removed the phone from his ear and held it against his chest. He glanced from the approaching sound of their pursuers and to face Allissa. He pointed right. Allissa looked at him, smiled, and then set off at a run down the walkway. A gust of wind whipped around them. Leo took one more glance at the hatch and then set off after Allissa.

His feet thudding over the boards, Leo caught up with Allissa quickly. The roof curved down before them, hemmed in by a series of boxy concrete buildings. A flock of doves enjoying the shelter of a rusting air-conditioner fluttered and cooed into the air.

The market's far wall came into view. Allissa slowed to a jog and then stopped. She peered down over the edge. A narrow alleyway ran down the side of the building, several stories below. The wall of the next building loomed up ten feet away.

"No, don't!" Allissa instinctively put an arm out to block Leo. He stopped, inches from

the edge, and reeled back, throwing a hand to his chest.

They both spun around to face the sound of raised voices which drifted toward them. The men charged up onto the roof and onto the walkway.

"What now?" Leo barked into the phone. "You've got us up here. You must have a pretty good plan!"

"Of course," the caller replied calmly. "Slide down the roof to your left and up onto the next apex."

Leo examined the roofs to their left. Sure enough, they connected at the bottom in the center. He glanced back at their pursuers. The leading man's face distorted into a mask of exertion and anger.

Leo scrambled from the walkway and down onto the tiles. Terracotta clattered beneath his feet. He leaned over and grabbed a board with his free hand.

"Quickly, now!" the caller hissed.

Leo let go and half ran, half tumbled down the roof. Tiles cracked and skittered beneath his feet. Leo reached out and steadied himself.

Boots thundered across the walkway nearby.

"This plan had better be good," he mumbled beneath his breath.

He slid to the roof's lowest point and leaped over a small drainage gulley, then scrambled up the opposite side. His feet slipped over the tiles several times, sending shards and dust careering downwards. He grabbed hold of the apex of the parallel roof and hauled himself up.

Allissa watched Leo with her hands on her hips. She glanced back at the men, cocked her head to the side and jumped. Landing nimbly on the balls of her feet, she ran across roofs and hurdled across the gully. With the grace of a gymnast, she caught the uppermost tiles of the parallel roof, and swung her leg over.

"Show off," Leo said, catching her eye and failing to quell a smile. He held the phone to his ear. "Now what?"

"Walk to the end of the roof," the caller commanded. "There, across the alleyway, just over six feet away, you'll see another rooftop."

Leo struggled to his feet and did what he was told. The boards on the summit of this rooftop were thinner and less secure than the last. Leo saw the roof that the unknown voice had indicated. He peered over the edge. The passage was narrow, but the drop was still disconcertingly far.

A strong breeze whipped in from the Bosporus, slapping Leo around the face. Leo wobbled. He extended his arms out in an effort to steady himself, then held the phone to his ear again.

"Get a run up," the caller said, "and jump onto that rooftop."

The meaning of the man's words sunk in slowly.

"You want us to jump across a six-foot gap? What about the drop?" Leo said. He removed the phone from his ear and eyed Allissa. "The guy wants us to jump," he said, the color draining from his face.

Allissa scampered across to the edge and peered down. Her knuckles closed around the tiles, whitening with the pressure. A flurry of debris drifted down the alleyway several stories below.

"No, we can't," Leo said. "It's too—"

"Listen," the caller said. "Calculating your running speed and the drop in elevation between the roofs, you can do it. I've worked it out."

Leo stared across the chasm between the rooftops, his heart beating at double-time. The gap seemed to stretch out before him like a yawning abyss. Behind them, the thundering footsteps of their pursuers grew louder.

"We have to jump," Allissa said, her voice tight. "It's our only chance."

Leo swallowed. His mouth felt as dry as sandpaper. Every instinct screamed at him to turn back, to find another way. Finally, he nodded, a sharp, jerky motion.

"Okay, let's do it," he said, finally conceding. He backed up several paces, his legs trembling beneath him. He took a deep breath, trying to calm the terror churning in his gut. He sprinted forward, his feet pounding against the rooftop, and leaped with all his strength.

For a terrifying moment he soared through empty air, the wind rushing past his ears, the ground far below spinning dizzily. Then his feet slammed into the opposite rooftop, and he tumbled forward, rolling to absorb the impact. The phone flew from his grasp, clattering across the tiles.

Leo swung around just in time to see Allissa make the jump. She soared through the air and landed in a crouch beside him.

"The phone!" Allissa said, lunging toward the device. The phone teetered on the edge for a heart-stopping moment before plummeting down to the street.

"We'll have to do without it," Leo said, scrambling to his feet. He turned to see the men run across the tiles and prepare to make the same perilous jump. "We have to keep moving."

"This way," Allissa said, pointing at a rusted fire escape clinging precariously to the side of the building. Reaching the escape first, Allissa half-climbed, half-fell down the metal stairs, the structure shuddering and groaning beneath her weight.

Leo followed close behind, taking the stairs two at a time. They reached the alleyway below, their chests heaving with exertion. The distant sound of shouting spurred them forward, and they ran towards the street, desperate to lose themselves amid the throngs of unsuspecting shoppers. They charged around a pair of overflowing bins and vaulted over a stack of discarded boxes.

Suddenly, a dark shape loomed in the passage's opening ahead. Leo and Allissa skidded to a halt, recognizing the man as one of their pursuers.

"He must have doubled back and cut us off," Allissa said, her voice trembling. She swung around, her eyes widening in horror as she saw the other two men clambering down the fire escape behind them.

17

Esin stared at a ship sliding along the Bosporus. The boat looked calm and serene against the chaos of the city. She swept her gaze in the direction of the Grand Bazaar. From the office she couldn't quite see the antique roofs of the world-famous market, but knew it was nearby. She imagined Balik and his men storming through the building and dragging those two interfering detectives, kicking and screaming, out of the way. Those amateurs could go right back to where they came from. This city was no place for them.

Esin spun on her heels and scrutinized the picture of Sadik-Tech's last CEO. Esin told everyone that she kept the photograph on the wall to remind them of what the company stood for. Ahmed Sadik had been a very ethical man—too ethical by half, in Esin's opinion.

She did not need to focus on the picture as the image was seared into her brain. In the photograph, the righteous idiot was laying the foundation stone of a new community center—paid for by the company's generous donation. That was a hundred thousand lira they would never see again. A sizeable chunk of money. Esin and the company could do with that cash now.

"Fool!" she whispered sharply.

Esin tapped the desk impatiently, her fingernails rattling against the wood. She forced a smile. Really, she knew the picture remained there to remind her to do what was necessary to succeed. Sometimes that was hard, sometimes it was dangerous, sometimes illegal—but, it had to be done.

Memories of that snowy night up in the mountains spooled through her mind. The look of shock on Sadik's face had been priceless. The man had not even considered her to be a danger. A sweet woman like her—he wouldn't have seen it coming in a thousand years.

Esin looked back out at the city. That night up in the mountains was the event that had set them on this course. Esin had stepped up. She had proved herself to everyone—the stuffy men on the board, the shareholders, to Sadik and herself—that she was not afraid to take decisive and lethal action.

She glanced down at her fingernails. The detectives should be in Balik's custody now. Esin's *decisive* and *lethal* action would soon see them out of the way, too. After that, it would be time to move on to the next stage of the plan. This was the most daring plan of her career. The stakes and rewards were higher than ever.

Esin glanced back at the picture. She would do whatever she could to make it work, and she wouldn't allow anyone to get in her way.

A knock resounded from the office door.

"Yes?" Esin shouted.

The mechanism clicked, and the door swung open. A wide-bodied man came into view. His sandy hair was closely cropped, and his thick neck strained against his shirt's collar.

"Mr. Fasslane," Esin said, steepling her fingers. "I trust you are as comfortable as can be in your makeshift home."

"You call that comfortable?" Fasslane spat. "I'm basically a prisoner in this place. I'm the most famous person in the world—"

"It won't be for long, Mr. Fasslane," Esin said. "In fact, I wanted to tell you that as long as we get our minor problem solved, we should be able to move out tonight."

Fasslane scowled, his jowls wobbling. "About time."

ALLISSA SLAMMED against the inside wall of the windowless truck as it turned a corner. Her shoulder bounced against Leo, sitting on the bench beside her. Allissa didn't know where they were going, but it didn't look good.

It was dark inside the truck. The only light came from a bulkhead lamp bolted to the ceiling. Allissa glanced at the dark patches which stained the floor and tried not to think too closely about what they might be.

One of the thugs slumped into the seat opposite them, his large frame twisted uncomfortably in the truck's cramped interior. The dim light inside the vehicle cast shadows across his rugged face. His eyes, cold and calculating, moved from Leo to Allissa and then back again.

The truck turned again. Allissa's head banged against the side. The truck screeched around a corner and picked up speed.

"Lovely ride, this," Allissa said, catching the man's gaze. He scowled and looked away. "First class hospitality. Can I leave a review online?"

Beside her, Leo remained quiet.

Allissa smiled sweetly, trying to dispel her blooming sense of worry. She glanced at Leo. Outwardly he looked calm, although she knew him better than that. She reached across and rubbed his knee in a gesture that said, *we'll be fine.*

The truck slowed, turned a series of tight corners, and then squealed to a stop. The engine idled. Footsteps approached the vehicle. One voice spoke, and another answered. Instructions were given in a language Allissa didn't understand. Then the truck crawled forward again. Allissa heard another noise, too. A distant hiss and whistle. It sounded mechanical, although she couldn't place it above the engine.

The truck rumbled on for a few minutes before pulling to a stop. This time, the engine coughed into silence. Allissa tilted her head and listened closely for any sound that might indicate their location.

One of the doors clunked open and footsteps thudded around to the truck's rear. The door swung open, and light streamed into the vehicle.

The man at the door barked instructions, and the sitting man staggered to his feet and shuffled out. The man at the door climbed in and slid onto the bench. He slammed the door, and the light faded.

Allissa looked at him closely for the first time. He looked like the classic thug they'd come up against time and time again. The black uniform of the National Police barely concealed his thick arms and muscular chest. His clean-shaven skin was so weathered it looked like bark. A thick scar ran down the side of his face, twisting his lips into a constant sneer. His eyes peered at Allissa, and then at Leo.

"Well, I'm glad that fun is now over." He pushed his knuckles together until his fingers clicked.

"What do you want?" Leo said.

"Straight to the point. I like this guy," the thug pointed at Leo. "Istanbul is a wonderful city, don't you think?" He looked down at his hands and then up at the detectives again. "You can get a beer, even smoke a bit of something if you want—whatever you feel like doing. That is a lot of freedom, yes?"

"Who are you?" Allissa said.

"Listen. For our citizens and our esteemed visitors to have all that choice, all that freedom, there are lines that cannot be crossed. Some rules that cannot be broken. Otherwise, the system, it..." The man made the gesture of an explosion with his fingers.

"I understand," Allissa said, nodding. Leo rolled his eyes.

"Oh, good, good." The man smiled.

"I understand that you're wasting our time," Allissa said. "Get to the point or take me to the nearest bar. Your hospitality stinks."

The man laughed again. He rubbed his right fist in the palm of his left hand. "Okay, okay, I can see you are... *sharp cookie.* I'll get to the point. We know you are here on tourist visas—" the man slid his hand into his jacket pocket and removed Leo and Allissa's passports.

"Hey, how did you get—"

The man raised the palm of his hand to silence the interruption.

"We also know that you are poking around in things that do not concern you. These things concern the freedom of the Turkish people."

"Rubbish," Leo muttered.

"We know that today you have been in contact with a known terrorist. A man who is an enemy of the state."

"I have no idea what you're talking about." Allissa shook her head.

The man removed a small audio player from his pocket. He poked a button. A few seconds of the conversation between Leo and the man on the phone filled the back of the truck.

"You have nothing to say about this? The man you are speaking to calls himself *The Guardian of Truth*. He has been a blight on this country for many years. He has caused protests, violence and even assassinations. Now, you seem like good people, but you're mixed up in something very bad here."

The man examined Leo and Allissa closely.

"I know that back in your country, you have a reputation for these sorts of *shenanigans*. Let me tell you, though, they are not welcome here."

The man banged on the side of the van and the door swung open. He issued some instructions, and an envelope was passed inside. He flipped open the envelope and passed a sheet of paper to Leo and Allissa.

"You have seats on the next flight back to London. It leaves in an hour."

Allissa glanced at the paper. It was a boarding pass for a flight to London Heathrow.

"You get on that plane, and I will never see you again," the man said, leaning forward and examining Leo and Allissa myopically. "If I do see you again, be warned that the Turkish justice system is harsh, particularly for terrorists." He shouted another instruction. Leo and Allissa's rucksacks were pushed into the truck.

"Now get out. Now!"

Leo and Allissa glanced at each other, picked up their bags and stepped unsteadily out of the truck. Allissa blinked while her eyes adjusted to the harsh sunlight.

A vast glass wall loomed before them. Allissa whirled around and saw, in the distance, the massive tail fin of an airplane. Their bags slung over their shoulder, the men pushed Leo and Allissa through a set of double doors and bundled them up a flight of stairs.

Leo and Allissa were shoved through another door and into the departure lounge. Allissa recognized the sound she'd heard some minutes before—a jet engine at take-off.

18

———

Leo and Allissa staggered through a group of passengers queuing for departure.

Leo glanced at the screen at the front of the line—*Amsterdam.*

Disorientated, Leo knocked the shoulder of a young woman coming the other way. Without a word, the woman continued, weaving her way through the lines of passengers waiting for their flights.

Allissa grabbed Leo's arm and led them to a quiet end of the departure lounge. A few passengers sprawled on chairs, reading books or scrolling through their phones. Through the window, an airplane lumbered soundlessly in the direction of the runway. A female voice spoke through unseen speakers, the words sterile and distant.

Allissa dropped her bag on one of the aluminum seats. "We need to stop and think for a moment." She paced up and down. "What's just happened? One moment we were at the Grand Bazaar and now we're here. What's going on?"

Leo dropped his bag next to Allissa's. He glanced around again.

"Wouldn't we normally have to go through all the security checks?" Leo asked. "Although I suppose the police can do what they want."

"If they *were* the police. I have no idea what to think now," Allissa said. "The guy on the phone said they were just dressed as the police, didn't he?"

Leo nodded. "It's strange that they brought us straight here. We didn't even go to the police station. We weren't formally arrested, nothing like that."

Allissa looked at a large screen on the wall in front of them. The screen displayed an image of a couple walking hand in hand along a beach at sunset.

"We've got involved in something that's way above our heads here." Leo slouched down beside Allissa. "The police, conspiracy theories—we just find missing people." His fingers tapped an erratic pattern on his knees. "How long until our—"

"We solve mysteries," Allissa interrupted. "And sometimes those mysteries involve governments, the police, whoever. There's still a mystery here."

"Where is Fasslane?"

"Who helped him disappear and why?" Allissa interrupted.

The image of the beach on the screen faded, and a news report appeared. A few short words summarized the world's headlines. Protests and riots continued on a global scale as the information in Fasslane's book found its way around the world.

"This is going to be trouble," Allissa said, pointing at the screen.

"But what can we—" The words dried up in Leo's mouth.

"I don't know, yet." Allissa tapped her lips. "Something will come up."

The news report faded to black. The screen remained black for several seconds and then a cursor flashed in the top left-hand corner. Then, appearing letter by letter, simple white text appeared on the screen as though someone was typing it into a computer.

You are in danger.

For a few moments the cursor stood still, blinking.

Leo nudged Allissa and pointed at the screen. His hands, which moments ago danced in frustration, lay dead still in his lap. He tried to swallow, but a lump of concrete had formed in his throat.

Another phrase appeared on the screen.

Those men were not police.

The cursor paused again.

Look in your bags.

The cursor blinked twice, and then the video of the beach returned to the screen. Leo and Allissa looked at each other, eyebrows raised.

"What was—" Leo's voice trailed off. He eyed the bag on the seat beside him.

Allissa was the first to move. She grabbed her bag from the seat next to her and tore it open. Her hands trembled as she rummaged through the haphazardly packed clothes. With each frenzied movement, a sickening feeling settled in the pit of her stomach. Suddenly, her fingers brushed against something foreign. She froze, her breath catching in her throat.

"There's something here," she whispered. "It's cold, and... sort of solid. Like a brick. It's pretty heavy too."

Allissa pulled the mysterious object to the top of the bag. The harsh, unforgiving light of the departure lounge cast an eerie glow on the white, plastic-covered, brick-shaped package. Time seemed to slow to a crawl as recognition dawned on her, a wave of horror washing over her body.

"That's some kind of drug," Allissa said.

Leo's mouth made the shape of the words, but no sound came forth. It felt as though the air had been removed from the room. The noise of the airport shrunk to a distant murmur.

With shaking hands, Allissa hastily stuffed the package back into the depths of the bag.

Leo sat motionless. The color drained from his face. He opened his mouth, desperate to speak, to say something, anything, but no sound escaped his lips.

"Look," Allissa said, pointing back at the screen. The video faded, and the text appeared again.

Leo. the writing came at the same speed as before. *Right trouser pocket.*

For a long moment, as though the events were happening to someone else and not him, Leo stared unmoving at the screen.

The text faded to black, and the news report appeared on the screen again.

"Quickly, look," Allissa snapped, shaking his arm.

Leo shook himself back into focus. He dug his fingers into his pocket as the text had instructed. His hand closed around a pair of wireless earbuds. He remembered the woman who had knocked into him as they'd passed through the departure lounge. He glanced around but couldn't remember what the woman looked like, even if she was still nearby.

Leo slid the ear buds from his pocket, wedged one in his ear and gave the other to Allissa.

"About time. Listen closely now." The caller's familiar

voice came through the earbuds as clear as day. "If you want to get out of there, you must do exactly as I say."

BALIK POUNDED his fist against the steering wheel as they waited at the airport security checkpoint. Beyond the chain-link fence, vehicles rumbled back toward the city. An airport security guard approached the driver's window. Balik rolled down the glass.

"Identification please, officer?" the guard said, his hands resting on the automatic rifle which was strapped to his chest.

Balik slid a hand inside his jacket pocket and produced a card. It was an expensive forgery, with the electronic record to go with it.

The guard took a cursory look at the card, then raised his hand to his colleague in the small cabin. The gate rumbled open.

Balik nodded, stashed the card back in his pocket. He powered the truck through the gate and back toward the city.

Watching the airport grow small in the mirror, Balik thought about the two detectives. They would be sitting now, bewildered and possibly scared, in the departure lounge, waiting for their flight. They wouldn't even see what was coming for them.

Balik pulled his phone from the pocket and dialed a number from memory. He held the phone against his ear as it rung three times.

"What?" came a gruff male voice.

"They are in position. Make the call. Do exactly what I told you."

Heavy breathing strained down the line.

"I am not an idiot, I understand. I do this and we are even. You do not call me again."

The line went dead.

Balik snapped the indicator, pulled the truck onto the motorway, and then placed another call.

"Is it done?" Esin's urgent voice came down the line. Balik imagined her sitting in the office, waiting for his call.

"Yes, it is done," Balik grunted, raising his voice against the rumbling truck. "The police will be with them in a few minutes. They will not be bothering us again."

"Excellent," Esin said. "Get back here as soon as possible. We are moving tonight."

19

"I know you'll have a lot of questions." The caller's voice was clear and crisp, as though coming from the next room. "I promise you that soon you'll get to ask them all. Right now, though, we're in a difficult situation. Did you check your bags?"

"Yes," Allissa said. "How did you know?"

"It's an old trick they've pulled many times. If they can't get what they want from you, they'll get *you* for something. Plus, it discredits you. People don't tend to believe the opinions of drug smugglers. I expect there will be something in the region of five kilograms in both your bags. By the time you get out of prison in, say, twenty years, this will all be a distant memory."

Leo paled further. His hands gripped the armrests.

"We're listening," Allissa said. "What do we need to do?"

"First, we need to get you out of there." The clack of typing keys came down the line.

"Not this again," Leo said. "No jumping between buildings this time."

"I'll do my best, but a team of the real police are already on their way."

"How do you know all of this?" Allissa asked.

"I have access to the airport's security cameras. I don't have time to explain properly now. Soon, though. Okay, remove any tags and shove your bags beneath the seats. Taking them with you will only slow you down."

Leo and Allissa nodded at each other and did as they were instructed.

"Okay, behind you, boarding for a flight to Amsterdam has almost completed. Gate 14. Without drawing unnecessary attention to yourself, get up and walk towards the gate. Look casual."

The departure lounge hummed with a quiet tension as Leo and Allissa made their way towards gate 14. Allissa's eyes darted around the room, taking in the handful of passengers still waiting to board.

"Good, get just a little closer," the caller's voice came through the earbuds, urging them forward. Leo and Allissa strode on as casually as they could. The attendant, preoccupied with checking boarding passes and passports, hadn't even glanced in their direction.

A new sound shattered the uneasy calm of the lounge. It was a noise that Leo and Allissa recognized instantly. The thundering of running feet, growing louder with each passing second.

They whirled around. A group of policemen burst into the lounge. The officers were dressed in full tactical gear. They fanned out across the room, weapons drawn and ready.

"Freeze! Police!" one of the officers shouted, his voice booming through the lounge like a crack of thunder.

"We need to get out of here," Allissa said.

"Yep, I'm monitoring their communications frequency," the caller said. "They haven't seen you yet. This should do it…"

A high-pitched squeal jarred through the terminal. It oscillated between two piercing tones. The once peaceful departure lounge erupted into a scene of pure chaos. Some passengers shuffled towards the emergency exits, others remained rooted to the spot.

The attendant at gate 14 snatched up the handset and shouted into the mouthpiece.

"Go now, through the gate. Now," the caller said.

Leo and Alliss charged toward the door. The airport attendant, now facing the other way, didn't even notice them pass.

Leo and Allissa ran down the ramp directly ahead of them. The door clanged closed, muffling the chaotic noise of the departure lounge.

Allissa glanced over her shoulder. No one else had made it through the door yet. They turned right into the umbilical corridor that connected the plane to the airport. Footsteps thundered on the metal walkway.

"Go through the door on your left now," the caller said. "Then, down the stairs."

Allissa and Leo pushed through the door and onto a metal staircase. Allissa glanced around them. The staircase ran down the side of the building to the tarmac below. Behind them, the aircraft sat ready to depart. The whine of jet engines filled the air. Several members of airport staff wearing high-visibility jackets completed their tasks nearby.

"Go now," the voice demanded. Allissa ran down the stairs, her feet clanging against the metal. Leo followed. Reaching the bottom, they slipped out of sight behind a concrete pillar.

Allissa listened closely, expecting to hear their pursuers closing in. She glanced around the pillar. To their right, the aircraft crew completed the final pre-take off tasks. To their left, a roadway for service vehicles ran between the terminal building and the airplane. The thud of a diesel engine approached from the roadway.

"There's a truck coming," the caller said. "It's going to stop next to you. The back door's unlocked. Get in."

A truck wheezed and spluttered to a stop beside them. *Alpha Airport Services* was just visible beneath a layer of dust.

Allissa peered around the pillar to make sure all the airport staff were engaged in their tasks. Satisfied no one was looking their way, she ran behind the vehicle and yanked open the door. The door was unlocked, as the caller had told them.

Allissa scrambled inside and Leo followed. She glanced around the truck's interior. Boxes and crates lay against the walls. Leo shut the door, and the light inside the truck sunk to a dull gloom. The engine growled, and the truck rolled forward. The crates rattled and slid with the motion. Allissa reached out for one of the walls to steady herself.

"A friend of yours?" Allissa asked, as the truck gained speed.

"Someone loyal to our cause," replied the caller. "Get comfortable. She will drop you where you need to go."

Esin stood from her desk and walked across to the window. The city through the glass had dimmed with the dying day. Lights on the streets and boulevards below shimmered in neon swathes. Esin looked out towards the Bosporus and the shores of Asia beyond. That's where they'd be heading in a couple of hours. From there the plan was simple—head out to her mountain cabin in Uludağ, where a fresh car and enough supplies for several weeks had already been prepared. What Fasslane did then was up to him. Esin would be pleased to see the back of him. Since he'd been hauled up here, all he'd done was moan.

After a short stay in Uludağ, he would probably travel overland and into the anonymous chaos of Asia, Esin imagined. Once there, he could be anyone he wanted, as long as he stopped being Brent Fasslane. The payments Esin had agreed to deposit in a private bank account each month would make that worth his while and reduce the temptation to go back to his old ways. The payment was just a small percentage of what Sadik-Tech stood to make when fear and unrest reached boiling point, and the government needed help sorting it out.

Fasslane was a loose end, though, Esin thought, studying her flawlessly painted fingernails. For now, he was a necessary one, but not for long. Loose ends had two options: they either got tucked in and didn't cause any further problems, or they got snipped off.

Esin dug her fingernails into the flesh of her thumb. She would give Fasslane the opportunity to tuck himself in quietly—he may be useful again in the future—or she would waste no time snipping him off.

The phone trilled from the desk behind her. Esin turned and glanced at it, glowing in the gloom. A fission of worry passed through her body. Despite the warm office, she shivered.

She strode back over to the desk and snagged up the phone. The call was from one of her police informants. She answered and held the phone to her ear.

"They've gone," came a breathless male voice down the line.

Esin balled her fists, digging her fingernails deep into her hands. "What do you mean, they've gone?"

"I don't have time to explain. I don't know how, but they've disappeared."

"What do you mean, they've disappeared?" Esin barked. Her nails dug harder into the flesh of her palm.

The line was silent for a moment. An alarm shrieked in the background and people shouted.

"I don't know. I have to go. I'll tell you when I know more." The line went dead.

Esin's lips curled into a snarl. She threw the phone across the office, smashing the picture of Sadik in the community center.

"Balik, why haven't you sorted this?" Esin hissed again, her nails cut into her palm. Sharp pain jarred from her hands.

She glanced across the office. The picture of Ahmet Sadik and the phone now lay amid shards of glass on the floor. Esin snatched up the phone and examined it. It was largely unscathed. She unlocked the screen and scrolled to Balik's number. A drop of blood smeared across the screen.

Esin paused and turned her hand over. Blood pooled in her palm from a small gash.

The photograph on the floor caught Esin's eye. Sadik smiled up from beneath the shards of glass, as though mocking her from beyond the grave.

20

The truck rumbled on for several minutes and then slowed. Eventually, with the hissing of brakes, it stopped completely.

"Security checkpoint," came the voice in the headphones. "Stay quiet."

A male voice, speaking Turkish, reverberated through the truck's narrow body. A female voice answered. The man and the woman exchanged several words.

"They want to look in the back," the voice in the headphones hissed urgently. "Get out of sight."

Leo glanced around. Daylight streamed through opaque panels in the truck's roof. He examined the racks and boxes, haphazardly strewn throughout the truck. He signaled to Allissa, and the pair slipped behind a stack of boxes at the front of the truck.

Outside the truck, footsteps thumped from the cab to the rear door. The male voice shouted again, more violently this time.

Leo turned to face the noise and missed a step, sending a pair of crates tumbling to the floor. The crash echoed, deep and sonorous, through the chassis. The footsteps stopped and a deep silence followed.

"I wish I knew what they were saying," Allissa whispered under her breath.

One of the guards shouted again. Finally, the driver's door clicked, and a pair of softer footsteps dropped to the concrete.

Leo took the next few steps with incredible care, then crawled in behind the stacked up crates.

The lighter footsteps had reached the rear of the truck. Keys jangled. With the truck's rear door being unlocked, the search for keys was clearly a ruse to buy Leo and Allissa time to hide. Finally, a key crunched in the lock and the mechanism clicked. The truck's rear door swung open. A flashlight beam swept inside.

Leo held his breath. He heard Allissa do the same.

A footstep clanged through the chassis as someone climbed inside. The truck swayed backward. Footsteps thudded inside the truck. The flashlight beam swung this way and that. A box fell and skittered across the floor. The hefty boots continued moving. The flashlight swept across the stacked crates and rested on the wall behind Leo and Allissa. The guard took another step toward Leo and Allissa. A box crashed to the floor, its contents bouncing around.

Leo's lungs ached, begging him to breathe.

The guard took another step closer. Leo could hear the man's breathing now. It was deep and rasping in the silent truck. The guard picked up a box and threw it across the truck. It crashed against the far wall.

A radio squawked, and then a distant, tinny voice filled the truck. The guard stopped searching. The flashlight beam dropped to the floor beside Leo.

The guard snapped the radio from his belt and barked

his reply. A tinny voice answered. He grumbled something unintelligible and then turned around and paced back toward the door. The guard climbed out and slammed the doors behind him.

Leo took three deep breaths but remained still.

A fist banged twice on the side of the vehicle. The engine whined, and they pulled away.

"We're clear," said the voice in the earbuds. "That was closer than I'd expected. Something has rattled them."

The vehicle swayed onwards, jarring Leo's spine with each bump of the road.

Leo took another two deep breaths and propped himself up against the wall. Allissa sat beside him. For several minutes, neither spoke.

Eventually, the truck banged and wheezed to a stop. The handbrake crunched, and the engine coughed into silence. The driver's door screeched open, and someone jumped to the ground. The locking mechanism of the rear door clicked, and the door swung open. Then light footsteps padded away.

Leo and Allissa looked at each other. Leo gathered his strength and climbed shakily to his feet, his muscles protesting with every movement. The uncomfortable journey had taken its toll on his body, leaving him sore and stiff.

He reached the door and scrambled down to the concrete. He turned, extending a hand to Allissa.

A narrow backstreet stretched out before them. Lights shone from the windows above and in the distance, the silhouette of a mosque's minaret pierced the skyline. Something scuttled in the darkness. A strong, cool breeze drifted past. Leo inhaled the distant scent of the sea.

"Where are we?" Leo asked.

"Sultanahmet, Istanbul," the voice in the earbuds replied.

"Back where we started," Allissa added. "Why are we here?"

"The answers are coming very soon. Walk to your right. There's a blue door."

Leo and Allissa turned and paced into the darkness. Metal shutters, no doubt loading bays for shops or restaurants, lined the narrow street. Something scurried beneath a dumpster and the sickly smell of rotting waste hung in the air.

Somewhere in the shadows, a door clicked and swung open. A rectangle of light appeared, revealing a small figure.

"Over here," the figure said. "Good to meet you. My name is Ramiz, and as promised, it's time I gave you some answers."

Leo and Allissa stepped into the bright light of a shop's back room. Ramiz, the man they had only known from his voice, was small, with quick features, and a head that seemed slightly too big for his body.

"Follow me," Ramiz said, leading them into the shop. Ornate rugs and textiles of various colors and designs covered every surface. Ramiz led them to the far end of the shop. A thick drape in red and gold covered the wall. Ramiz pulled the fabric aside and stepped behind it. Leo and Allissa followed.

The room was a textile workshop. Needles and threads covered a large table in the center. Tools hung on the walls.

"You make these fabrics here?" Leo asked.

"The man who owns this shop repairs them. He is an old friend of my father's, so when I was looking for a place to... you'll see... he suggested this."

Allissa picked up a stretch of red and gold embroidered fabric.

"There's a lucrative trade in antique textiles. The repairs can often be long and arduous, but they're worth it to see something like this enjoy a second life." Ramiz pointed at a small rug, depicting an elephant with a man on its back. "But that's not what we're here to discuss."

Ramiz leaned against a table in the center of the room and pushed. The table slid easily across the floor, revealing a hole in the center of the room.

Leo and Allissa stepped to the edge of the room and watched.

"I wasn't expecting that," Leo said, gazing down at a staircase, neatly cut into the floor of the workshop. Lights illuminated the hidden staircase, as though it were an exhibition in a museum.

"That's the beauty of it," Ramiz said, a smile lighting his face. "In the 1960s, my father's friend bought this land and set about building the new premises."

They followed Ramiz down the staircase, his voice echoing fitfully from the walls.

Leo focused on his footing on the uneven staircase. Sweat beads sprouted on his brow.

Ramiz reached the bottom of the staircase and paused before a door. Leo snuck a glance over his shoulder. The workshop had been reduced to a small circle of light. He couldn't estimate the distance they'd descended, but figured it was several stories at least.

"During the work they discovered this—" Ramiz drew back a bolt and shoved the door open. He stepped through, with Leo and Allissa just a step behind.

"Wow," Leo whispered, his voice sibilant. His eyes scanned the space, trying to make sense of it.

The roof, supported by pillars flanking both sides, arched somewhere overhead. The walls were constructed of large stones, chipped meticulously by hand. Giant slabs covered the floor. Leo took a step forward and pulled a deep breath of damp, cool air.

"It's a cistern dating back to the Byzantine era," Ramiz said. "It was used, alongside many others, to hold water, should the city ever fall under siege. People were very inventive back then. This is one of the smaller ones. We think it was probably built for a particular household who once owned this site."

"This place is amazing," Allissa said, crossing to the wall. She ran her hand across the stone and then rubbed her dry fingers. "And no one knows about it?"

"That's right, my father's friend considered opening it to public display, but seeing how many of the city's old buildings had been ruined by tourism, he decided to keep it quiet. I think he likes the idea that this is our little bit of old Byzantium."

"It used to be filled with water?" Leo asked.

"Yes, it was full when it was discovered. The draining tunnel, which leads down to the Golden Horn, was cleared out, and the inlet pipes have been sealed." Ramiz pointed at a row of metal plates high on the back wall. "There's an underground river sealed behind there."

"What do these mean?" Allissa pointed to a carving on the far wall. The indentations were worn into illegibility, but clearly made by hand.

"There are several stones in here with ornate carvings. These places were often made with recycled stone brought from one of the conquered lands. That could have been part of a temple a few hundred miles away. We don't know where for sure."

"Fascinating stuff," Allissa said, nodding and wide-eyed.

"But, you didn't come here to talk about fallen civilizations," Ramiz said. "We must discuss how we can stop our society from sharing the same fate. This way, please." Ramiz led Leo and Allissa to the far end of the cistern and tapped the keyboard on what looked like a top of the range computer set up.

"Now that's a cool set up," Leo said, examining Ramiz's four displays mounted on extendable arms.

"Wait a second," Allissa said, her arms folded. "Okay, so I admit I was a little distracted for a moment there by this amazing place, but we need some answers from you. We've been kidnapped twice and become international fugitives."

"You're quite right," Ramiz said. "Let me explain."

21

"We're here and will soon have the information we need," Balik barked into the phone.

Esin grumbled a reply, and the line went dead.

She was angry, and for good reason. The bumbling detectives had gotten away—that was not acceptable. Their presence threatened the plan.

Balik fumed. He had done everything right. It had all gone perfectly to plan. The detectives had been deposited at the airport, with enough contraband to do a lengthy spell inside. They should be languishing in a cell now, not rampaging through the city, intent on ruining things.

Balik snarled, tensed his arms, and strode through the office of the Istanbul Transport Authority. He approached a bank of screens, each showing a different part of the city. One of his men held the technician by the back of his shirt. Blood dribbled from the man's mouth and into his beard. The poor guy had chosen to work the wrong shift tonight.

Balik nodded, and the other man released the techni-cian. The young technician sprawled to the floor. Balik snatched him up, lifting him by the throat, and shoved him against the wall.

"You will help us, and maybe you'll live." Balik's hands closed around the small man's neck.

The technician nodded frantically.

"Once I have my information, we will be out of here. But... if you do anything to get in my way, you and your friends will be found floating in the Bosporus." Balik nodded at the other technician and the two-man security team. The three men stared back from the corner of the room, their eyes glassy with fear.

Balik and his thugs had stormed the office a few minutes ago and quickly bound and gagged them all. Hidden in the basement of a government building in Menderes, Istanbul's transport monitoring station was quiet at this time of night.

One of the security men groaned from behind his gag. Balik's thug stepped over and kicked the man hard in the stomach. The man slumped to the floor, wheezing.

"With your co-operation we'll be out of here in ten minutes," Balik said, examining the technician. Balik dropped the man into a chair in front of the glowing screens. "I need to trace a vehicle which left the airport this evening." Balik looked over the man's shoulder at the screens. The flickering images showed different parts of the city. Balik glanced at the control console.

"That could be several thousand vehicles," the technician muttered, his hands tapping at the keyboard.

"They'll have come from the airport's restricted area," Balik said, also giving the technician a time period to search.

The technician nodded. He tapped at the keyboard and images from the security cameras from around the airport filled the screens.

"Two vehicles left through the airside entrance during that time. A police vehicle, and a service truck." The technician pointed at the screen. "*Alpha Airport Services*, it says on the side."

Balik's hand crashed against the desk. He leaned in and examined the vehicle. "I need to know where this truck went. Can you do that?"

Just fifteen minutes later, armed with the information he desired, Balik shoved through the building's rear door and towards their waiting car.

"I AM IN A VERY FORTUNATE POSITION," Ramiz said. "Some years ago, I inherited a sum of money that allows me to follow certain passions."

Allissa nodded in a way that said, *get on with it.*

"In recent years, Turkey has seen an unprecedented rise in corruption. I don't necessarily mean corruption in terms of money. I mean the corruption of the truth. Sure, lies are told in the media everywhere in the modern world, but here in Turkey they are told blatantly, without any real attempt to cover them up. Our people are so used to it, so bored by it, that we just shrug and carry on."

"Five years ago, after an attempted coup tried to overthrow our president, largely based on lies and misinformation, I had to do something about it. So, I set up my small group of information vigilantes—*The Guardians of Truth.*" Ramiz pointed at the largest screen in the center of his desk on which a logo rotated slowly.

"We now have a team of journalists here in Istanbul and across the country who check whether the claims people make are true. We post the results—the truth as we have been, honestly and impartially, able to understand it—on our website and social media platforms. Clearly, this has not made me very popular with certain people. Fortunately, to this day, using VPN technology and other digital rerouting, I've been able to remain anonymous."

"Okay, that's one thing," Allissa said. "But spying on people using drones and hacking into the airport's security systems is clearly much more serious."

"Yes, this is the biggest operation we have ever attempted. When I heard that Brent Fasslane was about to speak in Istanbul, I knew there would be trouble. As you may know, relations between Turkey and the United States have soured in the last few years. Our leader does not like theirs, or something like that," —Ramiz shrugged— "but this man..." He tapped a key and a picture of Brent Fasslane appeared on the screen. "The egotistical maniac that he is, had managed to worm his way into the middle of it."

"The Americans wanted him back, but the Turkish government said no, right?" Allissa said.

"That's correct," Ramiz said. "There was some nonsense about a trade with a man of Turkish origin, but I think it's probably just a play of power. After a lot of nonsense, all both sides had managed to do was provide a man with a monumental score to settle the biggest audience on the planet. Everyone was watching him."

"And then he went missing," Leo said.

"Exactly." Ramiz pointed at Leo. "The Turkish blame the Americans, the Americans deny it all, no one knows who to believe. So, they turn to the blatant lies told by an angry little man." Ramiz turned back to the screen.

"Can one man really make that much difference, on a global scale?" Allissa asked. "Sure, this is embarrassing, but could it cause—"

"War?" Ramiz interrupted. "War is not caused by a single event. It's fueled by a growing mistrust, lack of communication, and then something pushes it over the edge. This may not cause an all-out war right now, but believe me, if we don't stop this man and whoever else is behind him, it will come. This is just the beginning. The wedge which he is driving between Turkey and America will force Turkey over to the great Asian powers."

"China," Leo said.

"We will again see a world divided in two. This is the biggest threat our society has faced in the last sixty years."

"Okay, okay," Allissa said, her palms out. "Let's not get ahead of ourselves here. He's just one man. A loudmouth idiot, I agree, but just one man."

Ramiz nodded. "He is one man who has already forced politicians from their positions, caused stock market crashes, and sent people rioting in the streets. He needs to be stopped."

"But how?" Leo said.

"First, we must prove that he's alive. Then we can start to show that his disappearance was all a front. All smoke and mirrors, as they say."

"I'm with you," Leo said. Allissa and Ramiz turned to face him. "I think we should out this dude as the trouble-maker he is, but how?"

Ramiz extended a finger and pointed at Leo. "Ahh, well, that's where I can help you. Take a seat." He indicated two chairs beside his own.

Leo and Allissa sat down. Ramiz tapped at the keyboard for a few seconds and a video filled the screen.

"Drone footage," Allissa said, watching the dark streets of Istanbul move beneath the camera.

"Yes, from the night Fasslane disappeared."

The drone slowed and then hovered.

"That's the Hagia Sophia." Ramiz pointed at the screen. "Each of these drones only has around thirty minutes battery life, so we work them in rotation, like shifts. This is the third one. Okay, watch now. You'll see Fasslane leaving."

Ramiz enlarged the image on the screen. Sure enough, a moment later, Fasslane and his guards shuffled out of the back door and around to the vehicles.

"Yes, we saw this from the security camera. He gets in one side of the vehicle and then straight out of the other."

"Yes," Ramiz said, shooting Leo a glance, "but did you see what happened next?"

Leo shook his head.

"They climbed through the vehicle, as you said. It's a classic trick. Watch what happens next." Ramiz tapped the keyboard to increase the brightness of the footage. Fasslane and his two security men ran to the back of the final armored vehicle and then scurried toward the gate. The drone followed them.

"There's the explosion," Ramiz said as the screen flared. The drone wobbled for a few seconds before steadying itself again. "Fortunately, the drone had already moved away from the vehicles by that point. There's Fasslane, look." He pointed at three figures, crouching in the shadows at the rear of the building.

"Wait for it. Look there." Ramiz pointed at the screen as a truck screeched to a stop on the other side of the fence. The truck's back doors swung open. Fasslane and his guards darted from the shadows and into the vehicle.

"Hold on, pause that," Allissa shouted, squinting at the screen.

Ramiz hit the space bar and the image froze.

"Can you back it up just a little?"

Ramiz prodded at the keyboard and the image juddered backward.

"Zoom in on that guy."

Ramiz did as Allissa asked and the image of the leading guard filled the screen. His face was set into a snarl of concentration, his jaw jutting forward. Ramiz changed some settings and the picture lightened.

"See the scar," Allissa said, pointing at the screen.

"It's the police officer!" Leo stated. "The so-called police officer who dragged us from the Grand Bazaar today. Do you know where they went?"

"Of course." Ramiz hit play and steepled his fingers. The police truck cut through the traffic away from the Hagia Sophia. Two emergency vehicles squealed past them in the other direction, lights strobing.

"If you know all of this, why can't you just reveal it yourself?" Allissa asked.

Ramiz paused the footage. "And lose my anonymity? No, I need to stay undercover. I need this to get out without anyone knowing where it came from."

"Couldn't you just give it to one of the newspapers?" Leo asked.

"This is too important. I need someone I can trust to deliver it to the right people and keep making noise until it's taken seriously."

Leo leaned back in the chair and thought about Marcus Green. He was just the right person to reveal this to the world. "I think we can help you with that. So, where does this guy end up?"

The truck on the screen wound through the narrow streets and then out onto the freeway. They accelerated into the evening's light traffic.

"Now, that's where this gets very interesting," Ramiz said, leaning backward.

At that moment, a slow clap reverberated around the cistern, followed by a deep peel of laughter.

"This is where you've been hiding, yeah. Underground, like the rats that you are."

22

Leo's heart leaped into his throat. He turned slowly in his chair.

Balik stood at the door. He tilted his head back and laughed again, the harsh sound echoing through the chamber. The jagged scar that ran across his face crinkled with each cruel chuckle. No longer wearing the police uniform that had served as his disguise, Balik now wore a loose-fitting shirt and jacket.

"You set us up," Allissa said, pointing an accusatory finger at Balik. "We'd be rotting in prison now if you'd gotten your way."

Standing behind Balik, two men with hardened expressions and bulging muscles cradled semi-automatic weapons. The sight of the firearms sent a chill down Leo's spine.

"That's the problem with our system, isn't it? You put on a uniform, and suddenly everyone trusts you. It is all too easy!" Balik said, tapping his knuckles against his chest. "What someone wears, is no way to tell what's in here."

Ramiz sat with his back to Balik and his men, his fingers flying across the keyboard.

"But this has worked out better than I would ever have imagined." Balik focused on Ramiz. "If my assumptions are correct, then you are the leader of the esteemed *Guardians of Truth*. You have been a frustration to my employer for some time. This is your secret headquarters, yeah?"

Ramiz stopped typing and turned around in his chair.

Watching closely, Allissa noticed Balik paused for a second. His eyes focused in on Ramiz, as though not quite believing what he saw. Then, his mouth twisted into something of a smile. He turned his attention back to the stonework of the ancient cistern. "You know, I like this place." He made a circle in the air with his hand as though physically searching for the word. "It's very fitting."

Ramiz, who had sat quietly since the intrusion, suddenly exploded with energy. He got back to the computer and hit the keys with renewed vigor. Images flashed across the screen. A loading bar appeared beneath the image of a padlock.

"Stop what you're doing now!" Balik screamed, pulling a gun from his hip.

"No way, you're not getting this information!" Ramiz shouted. "We will take you down with this!"

The loading bar crept from right to left.

Balik pointed his gun in the air and fired several shots. The gun roared, its deafening blasts echoing through the underground chamber like rolling thunder. Fragments of rock exploded from the ceiling, skittering and clattering to the floor.

"Stop it now, or I will shoot you," Balik shouted.

Ramiz tapped the keyboard several more times, his

fingers dancing over the keys. The screens flickered, then faded to black. He spun around in his chair, then stood up.

"Too late," Ramiz said, crossing his arms.

"Look at that," Leo said, pointing at the wall on the far side of the cistern. Balik's bullets had punctured the metal covering the cistern's old inlet. Water poured through the holes in narrow streams, splashing onto the floor below. As Leo watched, the metal covering groaned and then cracked under the pressure. The stream of water became a raging torrent.

"Take that computer, quickly," Balik said, waving towards Ramiz and the computer system.

The thugs rushed across the room, their footsteps splashing through the rising water. They unplugged the computer's processing unit just moments before the pool of water surged across the floor.

"We have some of the world's best hackers. They'll get through this in no time," Balik said.

"Let them try," Ramiz mocked. He stared hard at Balik, his eyes burning with intensity. "By the time you crack this, they will have shared this information with the world." He pointed at Leo and Allissa.

"I don't think so," Balik said, grinning widely. He pulled a smart phone from his pocket and checked the screen. "You see that? No signal."

"Wait, what?" Ramiz said.

"From down here, they won't be able to do anything." Balik barked instructions at his men, who promptly raised their guns. They stepped backward towards the door.

"And just to make sure you don't cause any more trouble, you're coming with me." Balik marched across the chamber and seized Ramiz by the arm. Ramiz yelped as Balik dragged him back toward the door like a rag doll.

Balik reached the door and turned back to Leo and Allissa.

Water covered the floor now, its surface glinting darkly. The old cistern, true to its purpose, was filling quickly.

Allissa stepped toward Balik and his men, water lapping around her ankles.

"You're really going to wish you hadn't come to Istanbul," Balik said, dragging Ramiz to the foot of the staircase.

Allissa looked from the steel door to Leo. She nodded almost imperceptibly. At the gesture, the pair charged forward, feet sloshing through the water.

Guns howled as Balik and his men fired into the cistern. The deafening noise boomed from the walls in a monstrous roar. Bullets thudded into the stone above Leo and Allissa's heads, sending shards of rock raining down around them.

Leo and Allissa ducked behind one of the pillars. They pressed themselves into the cold stone, their ears ringing from the deafening explosions.

Balik turned and then slammed the door. The crunch of the door's locking mechanism followed. Then footsteps retreated up the stairs beyond, joined by Ramiz's faint whimpering.

Allissa rushed up to the door and inspected the steel. There was no handle, lock, or even a keyhole on the inside. The steel was smooth and modern, obviously fitted when the cistern was rediscovered just a few decades ago.

She ran her fingers around the door's edge, feeling for a weak spot or anything she could use to pry it open. She traced the cold, unyielding metal but found nothing—no gaps, no loose panels. The door was well fitted and strong, designed to keep intruders out. She glanced back at Leo.

Torrents of water cascaded from high up on the walls. The water splashed onto the chamber floor, creating ripples that spread out in all directions. More rock fell away from the water inlet, pushed in by the pressure. The water gushed through with greater ferocity now. It bubbled and churned, rising with each moment.

23

___

"We need to make a full inspection of this place," Allissa shouted over the sound of the water, which had now turned from a murmur into a roar. "Ramiz said those stairs were carved out in the 1960s, right?"

Leo nodded, his face ashen, the muscles in his shoulders standing rigid.

"There must have been a way to get in here before that." Allissa looked up at the ceiling, looming far above them. "This cistern was here for hundreds of years. It must have had an entrance tunnel too." Allissa indicated the far side of the cistern. "You start over there. I'll take the opposite end. Look for anything unusual. A different type of rock, or something that looks as though it's been covered up."

Allissa sloshed through the water. It was almost up to her knees now and made moving about difficult. A cold shudder clawed its way up her spine.

As instructed, Leo splashed to the cistern's far wall and ran his hands across the roughly hewn stone. The cistern was constructed in large blocks of mismatched colors and sizes. Each would be too big for a single person, or even a pair of people, to move on their own. He glanced up at the ceiling, arching overhead. He took a deep breath in an attempt to quell his rising anxiety.

It didn't help that the cistern was lit only by a few spotlights in the center. Most of the walls lay in gloom.

Leo moved along the first section of wall, checking each stone in turn. No modern mortar indicated they blocked any tunnel or passage. He lumbered across to the next section of the wall, sending a wave rippling out and around the space. The water level passed his knees.

"Do you see anything?" Allissa said, her voice strained against the thunderous torrent.

"Nothing," Leo shouted, throwing her a look over his shoulder. "We've searched almost half this place now. Do you really think an entrance route could have survived all that time?"

"We've got to try," Allissa said, running her hands along the wall. The water rose again, lapping up and over her waist. Her teeth rattled, and she struggled to keep her hands from shaking. Preserved from the ravages of weather by the ground above, most of the stones here were as solid as they had been centuries ago.

"I think I've found something," Leo said.

Allissa spun around, charged across the cistern, turning the water milky white. Rising above her hips, it made movement difficult. Soon it would be quicker to swim. She reached Leo and put her hand on his shoulder.

"There, look, I think it's something," Leo said, pointing upwards.

Allissa squinted and saw what Leo was pointing at. Just below the level of the ceiling was the opening to a passage. It was about four feet across and square in shape.

"Brilliant," Allissa said. She stepped up close to the wall

and extended her arms as high as she could. The hole was about twelve feet above the ground and well out of reach. She scrambled up on to Leo's back, steadying herself against the wall. Leo helped her up until she was sitting on his shoulders. She reached up, but her hands still fell short of the opening.

"We're not high enough," she said, almost losing balance.

Leo wobbled one way and then the other before steadying himself on the wall.

"Stand up," Leo said.

Allissa struggled upwards, placing a foot on each of his shoulders. Leo grunted with the movement. Allissa stood slowly, walking her hands up along the rough stones. Toward the ceiling, the stones became dry and dusty. She reached her full height and extended her arms above her head. Her fingertips flailed around two inches below the lip of the passage.

"We're so close," Allissa said, straining upwards. Leo pushed up onto his tiptoes, the muscles in his feet and legs stretching to gain every inch possible.

Allissa gritted her teeth and jumped. Her fingertips scrambled against the rock, sending a cloud of dust out into the room. Shards of stone dug beneath her nails. Her fingers slipped, and she slid down the wall. Leo catching her before she fell into the water.

"An inch more and I would have made it," Allissa said, catching her breath.

Leo looked around, searching for something that could give the extra elevation.

A crack and splash echoed through the cistern. Another of the stones holding back the flow of water disintegrated and collapsed, crumbling under the relentless pressure. The torrent became a deluge, roaring into the cistern with a deafening fury. The water swirled now with such force that it was difficult to stand up.

"I'll get the desk," Leo said, pointing across at the desk on which Ramiz's computers had sat.

"Careful," Allissa replied, her voice sounding futile against the chaotic whirlpool.

Leo half swam, half walked across the room, the powerful current of the water threatening to sweep him off his feet. He and Allissa crashed into the desk, unable to see it beneath the turbulent water. A shock of pain jarred through his leg, but Leo ignored it. He reached down, grabbed hold of the table, and yanked. It didn't move. He tried again, pulling as hard as he could. His fingers slipped across the surface beneath the water.

"It's not moving," he shouted. "It must be bolted down or wedged here somehow."

Leo tried again. His hands slipped, and he tripped, falling into the water. His feet skidded against the stones as he struggled to get his head above the water. He found his footing, stood up straight, and his head broke free. He took a deep lungful of air. Water lapped against his neck. He looked back across the cistern. Allissa bobbed above the maelstrom on the far side.

Half swimming, half walking, Leo struggled back across the room.

When he was still a few feet from Allissa, another noise reverberated through the cistern—a dull click. And then, all at once, as though someone had simply cut the cord, the lights went out.

24

Esin rummaged in the cupboard beneath the sink and pulled out a dustpan and brush. She stood and looked around the small kitchen. The coffee machine ticked and bubbled, and the fridge in the corner hummed. Esin couldn't help but notice how outdated the place was—the walls were discolored, the counter chipped. A damp patch in the far corner threatened to spread across the whole ceiling.

When they landed this contract, an office makeover would be one of the first things she actioned. No, Esin thought, she would move them out of this old office all together. Sadik-Tech deserved to be based somewhere new, bright and modern. Set to be one of the biggest companies in the country, they needed an office space to match.

Striding back towards her office, Esin remembered how Sadik had rejected the call to move out to Ümraniye along with many of the city's biggest businesses. Sadik always said that he wanted the company to stay close to its roots. It was a company for the people, worked on by the people.

What an idiot, Esin thought, pushing through her office

door. A company for the people—now that was a recipe for disaster.

Esin crouched down and swept the broken glass into the dustpan. When the floor was clear, she picked up the frame and looked at the photograph. Shadows fell across Sadik's smiling face.

The phone on the desk behind her trilled, pulling Esin from her thoughts. Still holding the photograph, she strode across the office and answered the call. Balik's voice came down the line. It sounded as though he was driving.

"It has been dealt with," he said gruffly.

"Good," Esin replied. "Get back here. We move out soon."

"Yes boss," Balik said. "I have someone with me I think you'd like to meet."

THE DARKNESS WAS like nothing Allissa had ever experienced. A complete and utter surrounding blackness, it enveloped her entirely. It was so thick, it seemed as though she could just push it aside with her hands. She reached out, feeling the void press back against her fingertips. The air was heavy, almost suffocating, as if the darkness had weight and substance.

The water was above the height of her head now. She kicked, treading water, then turned and extended her arms. The wall was just behind her. Water splashed up on all sides —cold and black. The rough stones cut at her fingers.

Her feet kicked freely, keeping her afloat. She scraped around, looking for the passage they'd not been able to reach before. The circling maelstrom of water dragged her this way and that. She kicked and splashed, fighting her way back to what she thought was her starting position. Finding the wall, she dug her fingers in between the stones and attempted to tune in to the surrounding sounds. All she could hear was the white-noise howl of the pounding water. She heard a distant splash on the other side of the chamber and tried to turn towards it.

"Leo," she shouted, spitting water from her mouth. "Leo, I'm over here. Head towards my voice."

Allissa spat water again and listened for a reply. She kicked harder, attempting to fight against the swirling water and its attempts to drag her away from the passage. She sucked in a deep breath of cold, wet air.

She turned to the wall again and ran her fingers upwards across the stones, searching for the passageway. She tried to calculate the pace of the falling water and the distance they had to cover. The passageway would certainly come into reach soon, providing she was still in the right place.

A frantic splashing reverberated through the cistern again, closer this time.

"Head towards my voice," Allissa shouted again. The splashing continued. "Head this way," she yelled again, pushing her back against the wall. "We'll be out of here soon."

Allissa turned and ran her fingers along the stones. The crack she'd used to steady herself was now far below the water level. The water was rising quickly, clearly more stones had fallen in and increased the torrent.

Allissa extended her arms as far as she could, straining against the cold, damp air. Her fingers grasped the edge of the passageway above her, the rough texture of the stone grounding her in the moment. Relief washed over her in an overwhelming wave, momentarily pushing aside the fear and exhaustion.

She kicked harder, forcing herself upward and out of the water. Her fingers slid further into the space. She tried to hold on, to grip something, but the stone was worn smooth. The muscles in her legs burned. She slid both hands right and left, looking for something to grasp, but found nothing.

Finally, she located a fissure in the stone a few inches from the lip and slid her fingers inside. Just using her fingertips, she heaved herself up. Dragging her body from the water felt like a dead weight. Her arms shook and buckled. She tensed every muscle, grimaced, pulled herself clear of the water, and up onto the ledge.

A cool breath of night air drifted across the back of her neck. Allissa picked up the vague saline scent of the sea. She turned around to face into the cistern, sat on the ledge, and let the cool air of freedom slide into her lungs.

"Leo, where are you?" Allissa shouted, staring back into the cistern. "We need to go now. I can't go without you. Swim towards my voice!" Her tone wobbled with undisguised fear. "We need to go now!"

Allissa leaned from the ledge and listened to the sounds reverberating around the cistern. The splashes had stopped now. She hated to think what that could mean.

The water crept up toward her knees. Once it reached the ledge, it would pour, unstoppable, down the passage, possibly blocking their exit.

Allissa turned to the passage behind her. Warm outside air streamed across her face. Maybe she should go out there and get help. She could contact the emergency services and be back here in a few minutes, if Leo could hold on that long.

She tried to swallow, but her throat constricted. Her

stomach bubbled and writhed with the thought. She couldn't leave Leo, but she couldn't keep waiting, either.

"Leo," Allissa wailed. "Where are you? We need to go! Come here!" She gripped the edge of the passage. Allissa turned into the passage and took a deep breath. The water slipped higher still. It covered Allissa's fingers, just an inch below the ledge.

"I'm here," Leo said, croaking somewhere in the darkness. "Help me up!"

25

Leo scrambled, his muscles drained of energy, up into the passage. Allissa pulled him by the arm. He shivered uncontrollably as water poured from his clothes.

"We need to get out of here," Allissa said.

"Thanks for stating the obvious," Leo said.

Although Allissa couldn't see him, she could tell that he was grinning with relief that they'd found the passage.

"Let's hope this goes somewhere," Allissa said, extending a hand in Leo's direction. Her hand met Leo's shoulder, and the pair struggled to their feet, using the walls of the passage for support. The passage was four feet wide and five feet tall, meaning both stood up bend over, their shoulders pressed against the ceiling.

"This way," Allissa said, her voice loud in the narrow space. She extended a hand towards Leo. "Keep close to me. I don't think it's far."

As though in answer to their question, a gust of wind streamed up the passage, bringing with it the smell of the outside world.

Allissa led them forward as quickly as she could, feeling

out their direction on the passage walls. After a few steps, the passage began to descend at a steep angle. She slowed, placing each foot carefully in front of the other. Centuries of flowing water had worn the floor into a smooth and slippery surface.

Water bubbled and rushed across the stones beneath their feet, making the journey even more treacherous. The water level rose further, now streaming above her ankles.

A deep rumble vibrated through the passageway. The sound reverberating from the walls and shook the surrounding water. The temperature dropped a few degrees, sending a chill through their already tense bodies.

"What's that?" Leo hissed.

"I don't —" Allissa said, caught off guard by a sudden increase in the water level. She jammed her hands into the walls, the cold, slick stone cutting against her palms as she tried to keep steady. The water surged up to her knees, its icy touch almost paralyzing.

"Something must have collapsed back there," Leo shouted, his voice barely distinguishable over the roar.

Allissa pushed her hands harder into the walls on either side, wedging herself in place. The water dragged at her legs, each wave a battering ram threatening to sweep her away. The relentless current tore and ripped at the back of her legs.

"Take a deep breath," Leo shouted from somewhere behind her. "Let go when the next wave hits you."

Allissa tried to pull a deep breath, but the air was filled was spraying, furious water.

The wave felt like a collision with a juggernaut. Allissa's hands scrabbled against sides of the passage. Her skin scraped across the rugged stones. Water roared in her ears, deafening her. Then she let go. The water dragged her along, twisting her around and throwing her against the walls. She spun one way, then the other, losing all sense of direction, and speed.

Allissa tucked her arms and legs in close to her body, increasing her speed. She resisted the urge to breathe, knowing only water surrounded them now. Her lungs stung with the pain of inactivity. The torrent dragged her on. Distant bangs and crashes reverberated directly into her saturated ear drums.

Allissa crashed into something hard and suddenly stopped. She waited a few seconds before opening her eyes. The night sky stretched above her, backed by the orange glow of the city. She extended her arms and felt solid ground surround her. She dug her fingers into it and then drew another breath. This one came even easier than the last, although her lungs and throat ached.

She heard a coughing, spluttering noise from somewhere nearby.

"Leo!" Allissa yelled, rolling over. Her muscles protested at the movement.

Leo lay beside her, wheezing and coughing water out onto the ground.

Allissa blinked a few times, and her eyes strained into sharper focus. From the dull, ambient light of the sky, she saw that they both lay on a slab of concrete beside the Bosporus. Either side of them, the shoreline consisted of giant concrete cubes. The sea made a great sucking, whooshing noise as it moved between them.

Leo struggled into a sitting position and glanced behind them. The mouth of a giant pipe yawned a dozen feet away. Water streamed out of the pipe, running past them and down into the sea.

Allissa spat the last bit of water from her lungs and sat

up. She looked down at her hands, which were cut and scraped by the rocks.

"You're hurt," Leo said, shuffling beside her.

"I'm fine," she said. "They've almost stopped bleeding already."

Allissa propped herself up on her hands and looked out across the water. The lights of the Istanbul's Asian side glittered and danced on the inky surface.

Leo tilted his head one way, and then the other. His ears popped as water drained away. He could now hear the distant grumble of the city, the slurp and swoosh of the waves, the deep groan of a nearby engine.

Slowly, Leo came out of his daze, and the images of what had just happened scrolled through his mind. The cistern, the darkness, the rising water. He tried to speak, but the words caught in his throat.

A dazzling white light snapped on and swept out across the water like a curious finger.

"What's that?" Leo raised his head and looked out across the water.

A boat cruised slowly towards them. A bright searchlight mounted on the bow swept the surface of the water, encrusting each wave with a crown of jewels.

Leo and Allissa watched the boat, too exhausted to move.

The searchlight swept directly past them, forcing them to squint. The beam of light paused, and then returned, bathing them in stark white light.

Leo looked away, dazzled. He instructed his legs into action, but nothing happened. He was far too exhausted to move.

Allissa sat silently beside him, looking down at her hands.

Leo eyed the boat. Colors danced across his vision. The boat swung around and started in their direction. Its shadow merged into focus. The deep *thud thud* of the boat's engine cut through the noise of the water. A loud whistling sound emanated from the boat, followed by a click. Then a voice boomed over a loudspeaker.

"Are you Leo and Allissa?"

____

26

Leo and Allissa looked directly into the blinding light. Leo raised his hand to shield his eyes and nodded. "Yes!" he shouted.

"Where's Ramiz?" Although distorted by the speaker system, Leo could tell the voice was accented and female. At least it wasn't Balik.

"They took him away," Leo shouted in reply, unsure if his voice would carry across the water and the growl of the engine.

The voice didn't reply for several moments. "Stay where you are. I'm coming to get you."

The noise of another engine joined the boat's deep growl, this one high pitched. A skiff appeared from the stern of the larger boat and raced across the water. Powered by a small outboard motor, it skipped effortlessly through the waves. The skiff drew up to the edge of the concrete slab, just ten feet from Leo and Allissa. Water from its wake slapped the concrete, wheezing and whooshing through the gaps.

"Get in," the skipper commanded.

Leo examined the silhouette of the boat's skipper. She was slight, but precise in her movement. She knew what she was doing.

Leo and Allissa glanced at each other. Leo turned and peered back into the gloom. They had two choices—get on the boat with a stranger or fend for themselves. Leo listened to his instincts.

"Let's go," Leo said, struggling to his feet. "We can't sit here all night, and I could really do with warming up."

Leo and Allissa struggled into the skiff. The skipper revved up the outboard and sent them slicing through the water, back towards the imposing hull of the larger boat.

Allissa examined the boat as they neared. It was an executive yacht with a hull in dark blue or black. The upper decks were clad in wood. Most of the windows were dark, except for the bridge, which glowed dully.

Allissa glanced back at the skipper. The young woman swung the skiff adeptly in an arc behind the yacht. Her large waterproof coat rustled as she killed the engine and drew them gently in close to the yacht's stern. The outboard sunk into an idle patter.

Still without a word to Leo and Allissa, the skipper jumped to the yacht. She landed on the back deck and secured the skiff to a pair of large hydraulic arms. Leo and Allissa struggled out of the skiff, their legs wobbling. They steadied themselves on a railing.

"This way," the woman said, fixing Leo and then Allissa with a stare. She had bright hazel eyes and a wide smile.

Allissa paused as a strange pang of recognition moved through it. She had seen this woman somewhere before.

Leo and Allissa followed the woman up a flight of stairs and into the cockpit. The woman shrugged off the waterproof coat and hung it on the door. Her long dark hair, twisted into a thick plait, swung across her back as she crossed the room.

"I know who you are," the skipper said, turning with her hands planted on her hips. "But I'm aware that you don't yet know me."

The sense of recognition throbbed in Allissa's consciousness again.

"I'm Xanthe." The woman tilted her head to one side and looked from Allissa to Leo. Whilst she appeared to be Turkish, with olive skin and dark hair, her voice had an American intonation. "Ramiz is my brother."

Leo nodded slowly.

"We've seen you before," Allissa said, her voice weak.

"That's correct, I was in the Grand Bazaar." Xanthe now spoke with a thick Turkish accent. "You want fish hall, let me show you." She grinned. "I was in the airport too, but I don't think you saw me. You shouldn't have seen me, anyway."

Leo opened his mouth as though to speak. The words took several seconds to materialize. "You and Ramiz... work together?"

"Something like that, yeah." Xanthe crossed to the yacht's controls, her fingers dancing over the various dials and switches with practiced ease. "He's great at all the tech stuff. Get him away from his computer, though, and he's no good to anyone." She clicked the throttle forward with a smooth motion. The engine gurgled from somewhere far below decks, its deep, rhythmic pulse resonating through the hull. The yacht accelerated through the water.

"That's why we're going to have to get him back," Xanthe added. She focused on the horizon as she adjusted the steering wheel slightly.

As Xanthe expertly navigated the yacht back up the

Bosporus, Leo and Allissa accepted her invitation to shower and change. They returned to the cockpit twenty minutes later with an armful of snacks and bottles of beers from the yacht's well-stocked kitchen. Leo peered up at the glowing expanse of the Fatih Sultan Mehmet Bridge stretching across the water two hundred feet above them. The pounding tires of traffic on the Europe to Asia highway were inaudible from here.

"Feel better?" Xanthe said, turning from the controls and flashing them a smile.

"So much," Leo said, taking a gulp from a cold bottle of beer and then stuffing a handful of crisps in his mouth. "I can't believe... I'm still trying..." his voice trailed off as the sensation of the dark cold water lapped across his memory.

"How did you know where we were?" Allissa said, taking a ravenous bite from a chocolate bar.

"I got a silent alarm from the cistern. Ramiz must have activated it before he was taken. We'd always agreed that if he got into trouble down there, he would use that passage down to the Bosporus. I didn't expect you to flood the place, though."

"Sorry about that," Leo mumbled. "We couldn't help it... sort of."

"He's been working down there for years. I think he had the impression that it was so off-grid no one would ever find it. I kept telling him to be careful. I knew that one of these days they'd track him there, but he wouldn't listen." Xanthe's voice turned wistful. She spun the wheel, pulling them from the wake of a large freighter gliding in the opposite direction.

"How long has he been doing this?" Allissa asked.

"Ever since our father..." Xanthe's voice trailed off. She cleared her throat. "Ever since our father died, Ramiz has taken it on himself to be some kind of warrior for the truth. I kept telling him that you can't take on everyone, but he never listened."

Allissa watched the blood drain from Xanthe's knuckles. The freighter passed and the glassy black surface of the water settled down. Xanthe swung them back out into the center of the waterway.

"How long ago did your father die?" Allissa asked, her voice soft.

"Just over ten years. His car came off the road, up in the mountains. We were just teenagers at the time. The newspapers reported he was driving drunk, but Ramiz and I know that wasn't true. Our father never touched a drop. That's where Ramiz's crusade to stop the media from telling lies came from, I think."

Allissa nodded. She thought about her own father. Whist he wasn't dead, she hadn't seen him since the trial, during which her testimony had sent him to prison.

"He left us his share of the business in his estate, but before we'd even finished grieving, the other shareholders forced us to sell. One of them, a woman called Esin Kartan, did everything she could to discredit our father, just to get the business for herself. There was nothing we could do. We were forced to sell to them. I mean, we've never wanted for anything. I can't complain about that, but that business was his life."

"What did your father do?"

"He was a scientist, of sorts. His company created life-saving technology for health organizations. Devices that monitor vital signs, deliver medicines, that sort of thing. He even created a machine that can automatically restart the heart if the patient has a cardiac arrest."

The Istmarin Marina appeared on the left bank of the

river, a welcome sight after their tense journey. Rows of yachts bobbed gently in the water, their reflections shimmering.

Xanthe swung the wheel, her grip firm and confident, and slowed the engine. The yacht responded smoothly to her touch, the powerful hum of the motor dropping to a steady, quiet thrum.

"I'm sorry to hear that. It sounds like he was a great man," Leo said.

Xanthe smiled weakly, a fleeting expression of gratitude. She clicked the engine into its lowest register and the yacht slowed to a crawl. She deftly adjusted the throttle and shifted the gears to neutral, allowing the boat to glide gently towards the marina.

"He was," Xanthe said. She eased the yacht into place with practiced precision. "That's why we have to get Ramiz back and stop this madness."

"Where do we start?" Leo asked.

Xanthe jumped up onto the pier with agile grace, quickly securing the yacht with mooring lines. "Follow me," she replied, smiling.

27

"It is done," Balik said, shoving Ramiz into Esin's office.

Ramiz stumbled into the room, his hands taped behind his back and a sack pulled down across his face. He lurched around, twisting left and right.

"Have you totally lost your mind?" Esin asked, climbing to her feet. "I told you to get rid of them. Get them locked up, send them home, kill them. I don't really care. But I didn't want you to bring them here. What are we supposed to do now?"

The office was dark except for the light of the television and the turbulent illumination of the city below. Somewhere nearby, a siren shrieked and then faded, signaling that another night of violent protests was in progress.

"You don't understand, boss—"

"I think I do understand," Esin spat, interrupting Balik and marching around the desk, her hands on her hips. "You're the one who hasn't understood the most basic of instructions. Get rid of the detectives—how hard can it be?"

"No." Balik glanced at Ramiz, who was struggling to

stand up. "He's not one of the detectives. This man is responsible for all this," Balik said, pointing at Ramiz.

"Yes, so why is he not dead like the others? Instead, you bring him here. Get rid of him! Now!"

"I thought maybe you'd like a word with him, for old time's sake," Balik said, a mysterious grin lighting his face. He pulled off the sack.

It took Esin a few moments to realize what Balik was talking about. She looked from Ramiz to the photograph on her desk. Her eyes widened, and her hands fell to her sides.

"It's you," she said, pacing towards him. "You have caused us a lot of trouble."

Leo and Allissa dropped onto a sofa in the yacht's main living area. Allissa looked out at the row of vessels tied to the pontoon alongside Xanthe's. Most of the other boats sat in darkness, their outlines barely visible in the dim light. The occasional flicker of a cabin light or the muffled sound of voices hinted at the presence of others, but overall, the marina was quiet. The gentle rocking of the yacht and the distant lapping of water against the hull made the scene almost hypnotic.

Through the glass, Allissa watched Xanthe tie the yacht securely in place and then leap back on board. She landed soundlessly on the back deck and padded inside. She crossed the room and pressed a button on the wall. The electronic motor drew the curtains closed.

"How many gadgets does this boat have?" Leo asked.

"A lot," Xanthe replied, smiling. "You've met my brother, right?"

Xanthe pulled out a laptop and settled on the sofa opposite Leo and Allissa. "Ramiz sent me a video just before he raised the alarm."

"We were watching Brent Fasslane's disappearance just as those men arrived," Allissa said, glancing at Leo.

Xanthe tapped the keyboard. A wooden panel slid aside, revealing a screen built into the wall. The video started to play. She placed the laptop on the coffee table and sat back to watch.

On the screen, a police vehicle cut through the streets, the drone following from several hundred feet above. The drone's camera captured a bird's-eye view, showing the truck weaving through traffic with precision. The vehicle reached an intersection and turned left onto a freeway. The drone lagged behind for a few seconds, adjusting its position before swiftly catching up. The drone maintained a steady altitude and kept the truck in perfect focus, its high-resolution camera capturing every movement.

The drone followed for almost ten minutes as the truck weaved at high speed between other vehicles. The streetlights cast a rhythmic pattern of light and dark over the truck and the road.

"Those drones are impressive," Leo said, pointing at the screen.

"Yes, they are Ramiz's pride and joy. He designed the software himself. They work in a group of three from a facility in central Istanbul," Xanthe replied.

On the screen, the truck slowed and turned from the freeway, entering a narrower, more secluded road. The drone adjusted its flight path seamlessly, compensating for the change in speed and direction. It hovered momentarily, clearly recalibrating its focus to ensure the truck remained the central point of the frame.

Xanthe jolted upright and lifted her hands to her face.

The truck pulled down a narrow side street with tall buildings on either side. It paused briefly at the intersection before turning into an underground parking lot beneath a multistory office building.

Leo and Allissa looked at Xanthe, her face now a mask of shock. She pointed at the screen.

"What is it? What have you seen?" Allissa said, rushing to her side.

"That's... that's..." Xanthe stuttered. "That's the offices of my father's company."

For several seconds, Xanthe stared at the screen without moving, her eyes fixed on the screen. The drone hovered in place, its camera locked on the building into which the police truck had disappeared. The drone then backed away from the building and descended slowly, its camera angle shifting to give them a broader view of the structure's front. As the drone adjusted its position, a Sadik-Tech logo came into view, glowing prominently on the side of the building. The video feed cut out abruptly, and the screen faded to black.

Xanthe put her head in her hands. No one spoke for a few seconds. When Xanthe raised her head, her mouth was set in a determined frown. Her eyes burned with something close to fury.

"I don't understand why the company would be involved in this." Xanthe looked from the screen to Allissa and Leo. "Last I heard, they were working on projects for the government." She pointed at the screen. "I have no idea what business they would have with... what's his name?"

"Brent Fasslane," Allissa said, giving a short explanation of the man and the issues he'd caused.

Xanthe listened closely, and then summarized. "Basically, the Turkish government think it's the Americans, the Americans think it's the Turkish. Everyone else thinks it's a sign that the stuff in his book is true."

"Exactly," Leo said. "His disappearance is causing a lot of issues."

"I can see why my brother's involved," Xanthe said. "It's exactly the sort of thing he would get behind, particularly if it involves Sadik-Tech."

The three fell into silence again. The yacht bobbed forward and backward on a swell.

"We need to get your brother," Allissa said.

"If we find Ramiz, there's a good chance we will find Fasslane too," Leo said, trying to force a steady tone into his voice.

Xanthe's gaze moved from Allissa to Leo and then to the laptop on the table. For several moments she didn't move, her face clouded with thought. Then, as though suddenly deciding, she grabbed the laptop and tapped at the keyboard. A building's blueprint appeared on the screen, the intricate lines and details filling the display.

The document showed the building's layout in meticulous detail, including points of entry and exit, marked clearly with bold lines and annotations. The blueprint highlighted several floors, each with distinct sections labeled for various departments and facilities. Emergency exits were marked in red, and security checkpoints were indicated with small, shield icons.

"What are you looking at?" Allissa asked, leaning in to get a better view.

"After my dad died, I saved his files. Something told me they might be useful one day." Xanthe scanned the screen. She zoomed in on a specific area, revealing the basement level. The blueprint revealed a network of corridors and storage rooms, including a central control room marked with a star. Ventilation shafts and maintenance access points were also shown, offering potential routes through the building that could be less guarded.

Xanthe's finger traced the path from the underground car park entrance they had seen earlier, to the central control room.

"This is our way in," she murmured. "We can use the parking lot to avoid the main security zones. The executive offices are on the seventh floor. That's where my father's office was, and that of his leading team. There are meeting rooms too. He even installed an area for people to rest and shower if they needed it."

"And you think —" Leo started but didn't get to finish his sentence.

"I bet you that's where Fasslane is," Xanthe said. "My dad used to boast that the place had everything you need without setting foot outside. He provided all that sort of thing for the people who worked there."

Xanthe tapped the keys, and another blueprint filled the screen. This one detailed the layout of a particular floor. Leo looked at it closely. It seemed more like a luxury apartment than a commercial building.

"This elevator only goes between the seventh floor and the underground parking lot."

"That means people could arrive and leave without being seen, right?" Leo asked.

"Exactly. We need to go in there, get my brother and find out what's happening with Fasslane." Xanthe stood and paced to the window. She pulled one of the curtains aside and peered out. "And we need to do it tonight."

Leo and Alissa glanced at each other.

Xanthe turned. "Listen, I can do it alone, you've risked a lot—"

"No way," Leo and Allissa interrupted in unison.

"If it wasn't for Ramiz, there's no knowing where we'd be," Allissa said, standing. "We're not leaving him in there for a moment longer than necessary."

28

———

"If only your father could see you now." Esin stared down at Ramiz, who sat tied to a chair, his head bowed in defeat. Balik stood guard at the door, his muscular frame blocking any chance of escape.

"You're pathetic. Look at yourself," Esin continued. "You sit, day after day, behind the screen of your computer, causing issues for us all. You think you're this big guy with all these answers? Making the world a better place." Esin sneered, her voice dripping with disdain. She circled Ramiz like a predator stalking its prey, clearly relishing each moment. "Ha! You're nothing but an embarrassment."

Standing at the door, Balik shifted his weight from one foot to the other. He watched Esin and Ramiz closely.

Esin leaned in close, her face mere inches from Ramiz's. "Your father was the same, I suppose. He was a coward too, right until the end."

Ramiz blinked rapidly, his eyes glistening with unshed tears. A flicker of curiosity crossing Esin's face as she considered what it must feel like to care about someone that deeply. She quickly pushed the thought aside, her expression hardening once more.

"You know, I could kill you, right now, just like that," Esin whispered, her voice low and threatening.

Ramiz swallowed, his Adam's apple bobbing.

"I could do that, right now, just like that." Esin snapped her fingers, the sharp sound cutting through the silence like a gunshot.

At her signal, Balik pulled his gun from the holster, the metal glinting in the dim light. He approached slowly, his footsteps heavy and deliberate. He reached the prisoner and pressed the cold barrel of the gun against Ramiz's temple.

"But what would be the point?" Esin growled, her voice filled with contempt. "There's a certain glory in death."

She turned abruptly, her gaze drifting to the window. The city lights twinkled in the distance, oblivious to the drama unfolding within the office walls.

"No, I think you're better alive, at least for now," Esin said, a cruel smile playing at the corners of her lips. "That way, you'll continue to be an embarrassment to your family name."

She nodded to Balik, who lowered the gun and stepped back. "Let's go. We'll leave him here. A couple of nights tied to that chair will do him good. We'll see how he feels when we get back."

With that, Esin strode out of the room. Balik followed close behind, leaving Ramiz alone in the darkness.

Down in the parking lot, Esin led Balik and Fasslane across to a BMW X5. The dim, fluorescent lights overhead cast long shadows through the vast underground space. Balik pulled the key from his pocket and unlocked the car, a high-pitched beep piercing in the stillness.

Fasslane pulled open one of the rear doors and shuffled

inside, the leather seats creaking under his weight. Esin slid into the passenger seat, her eyes scanning the lot for any sign of movement.

Balik got into the driver's seat and the BMW's engine roared to life with a deep and powerful growl. The lights blazed, cutting through the gloom.

Balik clicked the vehicle into reverse and pulled out of the bay, the tires crunching over the concrete. They barreled up the ramp, the engine's growl echoing off the walls, and emerged into the evening air.

Esin glanced out of the window, her eyes drawn to the looming silhouette of the Sadik-Tech building. They were now on the home straight. Within the hour Fasslane would be out of Istanbul, and then no one could prevent the chaos. As they sped away into the night, a smile spread across her face.

XANTHE'S all electric Toyota BZ4X whispered down the fast lane of the freeway, overtaking a lumbering truck which spewed clouds of smoke into the already saturated city air.

Reclining in the passenger seat, Leo examined the controls. Details about their location, speed, and the running of the vehicle showed on a large screen on the center console. Beside him, Xanthe gripped the tiny steering wheel, which looked to Leo like something from a fighter jet. Leo turned back to the screen and looked at the clock— it was approaching 2am. He tried to piece together the events of the day. Only twelve hours had passed since their mysterious meeting at the Grand Bazaar. It felt like days ago. He stifled a yawn and glanced at Allissa in the back seat. She looked tired too.

The Sea of Marmara stretched out to their left, murky and featureless. Only the ships which waited at anchor, or sluggishly slipped through the oil-colored night, their lights spewing across the water, broke the monotony.

Xanthe indicated and swung the Toyota onto an exit ramp. Without slowing, she took a right, then a left turn, the tires screeching across the asphalt. Restaurants and shops flashed past, all shut up for the night. Metal shutters covered the windows of some, others were boarded up against the violence and protests that had swept through the city. Dozens of signs in countless languages shouted for attention.

The Toyota screeched around a junction. Leo glanced anxiously to the right. He was glad to see the road was empty. Parked cars lay dormant on each side of the carriage-way. Two had their windscreens smashed in and one was charred by flames.

The occasional light glowed from concrete apartment buildings on either side of the road. Most windows were unlit.

If you wanted to smuggle something or someone out of the city, this would be the perfect time to do it, Leo thought.

Xanthe swung the wheel, and the Toyota screeched into a side street.

"Shortcut," Xanthe shouted.

Metal stairwells zigzagged up concrete walls on either side. Washing, stiff and forgotten, hung between the build-ings, swaying slowly in the breeze. They cruised past several overflowing dumpsters. A family of tabby cats examined the silent vehicle from behind piles of rubbish.

"We're going to find him, you know?" Leo said, his voice loud against the silent vehicle. "There's no need to worry about that at all."

Xanthe's eyes flicked from the road to Leo. She smiled weakly and lessened her pressure on the accelerator.

"He's the only family I've got," Xanthe said after a few seconds' silence.

Leo nodded. "You're not losing him tonight."

"And we're going to solve this," Allissa said, as they passed a restaurant, its windows smashed. "We need to expose this guy for the fraud he is."

Leo nodded.

"I hope so," Xanthe said, looking forlorn. "I really hope so..." Her voice trailed off, before she yelled, "There it is!"

She swung the Toyota around a tight corner. Leo peered up at the glass and concrete building. Set back from the road, and fronted by a wide, grand plaza, the tower occupied the entire city block. Whilst it was only seven stories in height, it dwarfed its neighbors.

"I thought you said it had sea views?" Leo said, looking at the jumble of mismatched buildings which surrounded them on all sides.

"You can from the seventh floor." Xanthe pointed towards the upper floors. "My father resisted the pressure to move to Ümraniye as the business grew. He saw this as his home, as well as that of the business."

Xanthe slowed the Toyota and turned towards the underground parking lot. Above them, the Sadik-Tech logo glowed ominously from the side of the building, casting a blood-red hue over the surroundings.

The Toyota swept down the ramp. The dim lights overhead flickered, casting eerie shadows on the concrete walls. Xanthe momentarily slowed as a barrier came into view. Then, with a determined grumble, she hit the accelerator. The Toyota shot forward, smashing into the barrier. The barrier snapped clean off upon impact, skittering and clattering across the parking lot.

"Won't they know we're coming?" Allissa said.

"Maybe," Xanthe replied, her tone unwavering. She hit the brakes hard, sending them into a controlled skid. The sound of screeching tires reverberated through the space. She brought the car to a stop and killed the lights, plunging them into near darkness. They all got out of the car and looked around. The parking lot appeared to be empty.

Wearing black sports clothes that hugged her athletic frame, Xanthe looked every bit the part of an action movie heroine. Allissa couldn't help but compare her to a character from one of those high-stakes thrillers. She certainly was fearless enough to play the role.

"I don't care if they know we're coming," Xanthe said. "I'm ready."

29

———

Xanthe strode to rear of the Toyota and opened the trunk. A light snapped on. She rummaged through a black duffel bag and extracted three flashlights. She gave Leo and Allissa one each, then swung the bag onto her back.

"Is this all we've got?" Allissa said, looking at the flashlight. "They'll be armed for sure."

Leo weighed up the flashlight and thought about how they'd faced people with guns before and survived.

"Yep," Xanthe said, slamming the trunk closed. "My father was against weapons. We have everything we need here." She tapped the side of her head. "Keep the lights off for now. Follow me."

Xanthe led them across the parking lot. Darkness swamped large areas of the underground space. A fluorescent bulb flickered on the far side, casting strange and wraithlike shadows across the concrete.

Several vehicles, including the police van, two armored vehicles and a couple of luxury civilian cars, sat against the far wall.

Xanthe paused and dug a phone from her pocket. She tapped the screen and one of the building's schematics appeared. Her fingers darted around, finding the part she required. "This way," she said finally, leading them on.

Xanthe reached a door in the far corner.

Danger electricity. Do not enter, read a sign in Turkish, and below in English.

Xanthe twisted the handle and pulled. The door shuddered against its fixings but didn't open.

"No matter," Xanthe muttered, pulling the bag from her back. She rummaged around inside and removed a small pry bar.

"That could totally be used as a weapon," Leo said sarcastically.

"No, this is a tool," Xanthe retorted, grinning. She shoved the bar between the door and the jamb, then heaved it with surprising force. The door popped free of its lock. Xanthe snapped on the flashlight. A large array of electrical equipment blinked from the far wall of a small room. She strode over to the master breaker and pulled down the switch. A dull clang resonated through the room. The building fell into total darkness.

"This way," Xanthe said, leading them back across the car park. A couple of emergency lights shone from near the exits, the rest of the floor lay shrouded in darkness.

Leo clicked his flashlight on. A finger of light swept through the space and rested on a set of double doors at the far end.

They doubled their pace towards the doors and pushed through into a stairwell.

"Why aren't these doors locked?" Alissa asked, eying the mag-lock system mounted at the top of each door.

"No power," Xanthe said, grinning. "It looks like they haven't upgraded since my father died. This company isn't as profitable as it appears. Seventh floor."

Xanthe led them up the stairs, their footsteps hammering on the bare concrete steps. Pipes and electrical cables ran up the walls. Aside from the three fingers of light, sweeping haphazardly from their flashlights, the darkness was absolute.

Leo's pulse quickened with the climb. As fit as he was, by the fifth floor his heart pounded. On the sixth floor, Xanthe paused. She leaned over the railing and then peered up at the floors above them.

Leo caught his breath and tried to quell the rising, sickening sense of unease. He peered through the glass panel on the door into the sixth floor. Two emergency lights were the only distinguishable features on the entire level.

"I remember coming here as a child," Xanthe said, as Allissa caught up, panting. "My father's team used to treat us like celebrities. They'd spoil us, take turns in looking after us. Back then, I thought they were just nice people. That all changed after he died."

"People can be two faced," Allissa said, catching her breath. "Especially when money's involved."

Refreshed from the pause, the three charged up the stairwell. Xanthe reached the landing a few steps ahead of the others. She peered through the door's glass panel. This floor, like those below, was unlit.

Leo and Allissa joined her a moment later. The three stood stationary, listening.

"I can't hear anything," Allissa said. "If Ramiz is here, then—"

Xanthe charged forward, panic etched across her face.

"We go in together," Allissa said, grabbing Xanthe by the arm. "We have no idea what we're going to find in there."

Xanthe pulled a deep breath, her muscles tense.

"You're no good to anyone dead," Leo said, instantly regretting his harsh word choice. "Let's go, in three, two..."

They charged through the door together, senses on high alert. Leo took two steps, fanned out to the left, and paused. His flashlight swept the room in front of him, the beam cutting through the gloom. As Xanthe had described, the office was sumptuously furnished. Leather sofas squatted in the dimness, their shapes distorted by the shadows. Large plants cast eerie silhouettes on the walls, their leaves casting finger-like shadows. Downtown Istanbul glowed through the windows, the inky blanket of the sea stretching out beyond.

Xanthe ran into the middle of the space, her footsteps muffled by the carpet. Allissa took the right side, her flashlight beam sweeping erratically over desks and chairs.

The whole building was as silent as a grave.

Leo reached a row of doors with glimmering brass plaques. Executive offices, he assumed.

"In here, maybe," Leo whispered. He approached the first door and depressed the handle. The mechanism clicking. The door wasn't locked. He shoved the door open. The door creaked and swung inwards, the sound jarring through the silence. He stepped inside and panned the flashlight around the office, checking every corner. The room was empty, the air stale. More than empty though, Leo thought, the place looked abandoned. There were no photographs on the desks, no papers in trays, no books on the shelves.

He exhaled and stepped back into the outer office. He tried the next three doors but found each of them empty. All the executive offices were deserted, the once luxurious furnishings now nothing more than ghosts. Allissa and Xanthe joined him as he approached the final door.

"Find anything?" Leo asked, already knowing the answer.

Both shook their heads, their eyes showing fear and uncertainty.

"The place is empty," Xanthe whispered, her voice trembling slightly. "It's like no one's been here in ages."

Leo, Allissa, and Xanthe raised their flashlights, three beams of light converging on the final door like spotlights on a stage. Xanthe approached the door, her hand shaking as she reached for the handle. She pushed down, the lock disengaging with a soft click. She swung the door open.

Xanthe, Allissa, and Leo stepped inside, then froze in their tracks. Their flashlight beams converged on an object in the middle of the room. Tied to a chair, his eyes wide and fear-filled, sat Ramiz. His face was pale and gaunt in the harsh glare of the flashlights.

Xanthe charged forward, her voice urgent and desperate as she spoke to Ramiz in a language Leo didn't understand. Xanthe slid out a knife and cut the bindings quickly.

Ramiz turned and looked up at them, his gaze darting between their faces. He winced in pain, his breath coming in short, ragged gasps as the ropes fell away.

"Are you hurt?" Allissa asked, sweeping her light across his body, searching for any sign of injury.

Ramiz shook his head, his movements slow and sluggish, as if every motion caused him great effort.

Ramiz rubbed at his wrists, the skin raw and chafed from the bindings. He slumped further into the chair.

"They have Fasslane," he said, his voice hoarse. He took an unsteady step forward, his legs trembling beneath him, and hugged Xanthe. "They're planning to escape tonight. They've got an exit strategy planned. A place somewhere in the east where he'll lie low for a few months until this all blows over."

Through the window, the city glittered in the hazy night, the lights twinkling like stars in the vast expanse of the sky. The thick, dark smudge of the Bosporus loomed, spanned by the Fatih Sultan Mehmet Bridge, its cables stretching across the water like the threads of a spider's web.

"You can go on the record and tell everyone what you know, and blow this thing wide open," Allissa said, her voice urgent and insistent.

"No, that won't work," Ramiz said. "That'll just add fuel to the fire. We need proof. Proper, irrefutable evidence."

Leo nodded, his mind racing with possibilities. "How can we get that?"

Ramiz stared at something through the window, his eyes distant and unfocused, as if seeing something that no one else could. He didn't reply, lost in his own thoughts.

"Ramiz?" Allissa said, her voice cutting through the silence. "What do we do? We need to stop them and expose Fasslane for the liar he is."

Without answering, Ramiz spun around to face his sister.

"Did you bring your laptop?" Ramiz asked, his voice tight with anticipation.

"Yes, of course. It's in the car," Xanthe replied, her brow furrowed in confusion.

"Excellent," Ramiz said, spinning to face Leo and Allissa, his eyes gleaming with a newfound sense of purpose. "Then we go after them ourselves."

"But we don't know where they're going, do we?" Leo said.

Ramiz and Xanthe had already set off across the office, their footsteps echoing in the empty space.

Leo turned back to look at Allissa, her silhouette stark against the glittering backdrop of the city. She shrugged, her eyes meeting his in a moment of shared understanding, and then ran after Ramiz and Xanthe.

30

Xanthe unlocked the car as they approached and then hopped into the driver's seat. Ramiz slid into the passenger seat beside her.

"Under the seat," Xanthe said, before Ramiz could even ask.

Ramiz bent over and pulled out a laptop. He cracked it open on his knees and fired it up.

Leo and Allissa scrambled into the back seats.

Xanthe started the car. It hummed gently as the electric motors warmed up.

"Where are we going?" Xanthe said, turning to face her brother.

"One moment," Ramiz said, his fingers flying over the keyboard. "I'm just getting the details of the vehicle they used."

Leo peered around the seat and saw that Ramiz was scrolling through footage from the building's security cameras.

"I suppose you've used some cutting-edge tech to hack through their defenses and get that?" he said.

Allissa rolled her eyes.

Ramiz glanced up at him. "No, I just logged in. They haven't changed the password since our dad died. It's actually his date of birth," Ramiz replied, deadpan. "This next part is a bit trickier, though, and slightly more illegal. They're in a BWM X5. There's no record of it on the company system, unless... ahhh! There we are!" He pointed at the screen and bounced up and down in excitement.

Xanthe tapped impatiently on the steering wheel.

"It's leased from a company in Başakşehir, and wait a minute... yes, they do! Yes, they do!"

"He's always like this," Xanthe said, turning and shrugging apologetically at Leo and Allissa. "It'll make sense in a minute, when the rest of the world catches up."

Ramiz tapped at the keyboard again, and a map of Istanbul materialized. A few moments later, a pulsing blue dot appeared.

"There they are," Ramiz said, triumphantly pointing at the screen. "Turn left."

"How did you—" Leo said.

"It's best not to—" Xanthe interrupted, clicking the car into drive, and accelerating toward the exit ramp.

"Lease companies often install trackers in their vehicles in case of theft. Sure, BMWs have their own system, which you can piggyback, but their encryption is like, you know, sigma grade stuff. The lease companies..."

Leo caught Allissa's eye and made a mental note not to ask Ramiz about technical things again.

"What now?" Xanthe asked as they swung out of the parking lot and sped north.

"They're heading toward the Asian side. They've just joined the E80 heading east. It's always been their plan to get Fasslane away from here. In no time they'll be out in rural Turkey. I expect they'll switch vehicles as soon as they're out of the city, and then we'll lose the trace."

Leo sank back into the seat, his mind racing as he tried to think through their options. In every case so far, they had managed to find some way to get ahead, to stay one step ahead of their adversaries. It was like solving a complex puzzle, each piece falling into place as they uncovered new information and insights. The key to their success lay in understanding the person on the other side, in getting inside their thoughts and feelings.

Ramiz typed furiously, a look of anguish clouding his face.

"Hold on a minute," Leo said, leaning forward, his gaze intense and focused. "What are they most afraid of?"

"What do you mean?" Xanthe asked, passing through an intersection without slowing.

"If we know what they're most afraid of, we can try to understand their plan, or at least how to—"

"Fasslane being exposed as a liar," Ramiz said. "If there is clear, irrefutable evidence that Fasslane hasn't been taken by the Americans, or murdered by some secret society, then that disproves all of his claims."

"That's right!" Xanthe said excitedly. "Without that, his book is just a load of nonsense."

"And without that, Esin's business won't get its way with the ministry of defense and Fasslane will be seen as the idiot he actually is," Ramiz continued.

Allissa nodded. "But it would need to be in plain sight, for the whole world to see."

"There." Leo leaned forward and pointed at the map on the screen. "I think I've got a plan, and we need to do it right there."

As the brightly lit curve of the E80 freeway came into view, Leo explained his plan. The others listened in silence.

"I know just the people to help," Ramiz said when he'd finished, typing quickly.

~

THE BMW X5 roared down the highway as Balik pushed the pedal to the floor. The illuminated towers of the Fatih Sultan Mamet Bridge loomed ahead, their lights piercing the darkness like beacons. Balik scanned the traffic behind them, his eyes darting from car to car, searching for any sign that they were being followed. The road at this hour was almost deserted. The only sound was the wind whistling past the windows and the growl of the engine.

"Slow down," Esin hissed from the passenger seat, her voice tight with tension. "We all want to get there as soon as possible, but we can't draw attention to ourselves. Especially with him—" she nodded towards Fasslane in the backseat, his face a mask of fear as he stared out the window. "Stay below 55."

"No one's following, boss. It's okay. We are alone," Balik replied, his voice steady. He glanced in the mirror again. The distant headlights of disinterested vehicles winked in and out of view like fireflies in the night. Nothing was close enough to be a threat.

"I don't care what you think you know," Esin snarled, her voice venomous. "Reaching our destination a few minutes sooner is not worth the risk. We're not ruining the plan now, not when we're so close."

Balik glanced at the woman beside him, her short bob-cut swinging about her face as she turned to look out of the window. He took a deep breath and eased his foot off the gas. The X5 slowed, the engine's roar fading to a soft purr. He rolled his shoulders, trying to loosen the knot of tension that had taken up residence in the center of his back. He eyed Fasslane sitting rigidly in the backseat, his face a mask of apprehension. Beads of sweat glistened on his forehead, and his eyes darted nervously from side to side, as if expecting danger to materialize at any moment.

"It's okay," Esin muttered quietly, as though trying to convince herself. "The plan is flawless. We will be in Uludağ in a couple of hours. Then we'll have vanished before anyone gets the chance to follow us." She turned to face Balik, her piercing gaze boring into him. "You do not believe me?"

"Of course I believe you, boss," Balik said, nodding soberly.

They sped onto the Fatih Sultan Mehmet Bridge, the iconic structure bathed in a mesmerizing purple glow against the inky blue-black sky. The lights of Asian Istanbul danced tantalizingly close, their reflections shimmering on the surface of the waters of the Bosporus. A lone freighter slipped beneath the bridge, heading for the Red Sea.

"You see," Esin said, as though crossing the bridge signified their freedom. "You have nothing to worry about. We'll be there soon, and then he can disappear." She pointed a thumb at Fasslane. "Once he's gone, there is nothing to incriminate us."

A set of bright headlights caught Balik's eye in the mirror. He glanced at it, his heart skipping a beat. Something was approaching them quickly in the right-hand lane, the roar of its engine growing louder with each passing second. The lights drew closer, their glare dazzling him. He glanced at Esin, who turned to see the vehicle approaching.

"It's nothing," she said, reading the worry in his face. "Some idiot showing off. Let them pass. No problem."

Balik kept the X5 steady, his knuckles tensing on the steering wheel. The lights neared, splitting from two into six, and he squinted in the mirror. If he wasn't mistaken, three large vehicles were gaining on them at over eighty.

The BMW passed bridge's center point, the thick cables that suspended the roadway flashing by in a stream of color before rising to meet the tower on the far side. The lights of the opposite bank, a blur of white and orange, were almost upon them now.

Balik eyed the mirror again. The bright lights of the approaching vehicles closed in, causing colors to dance across his vision. The rumble of several nearby engines rose above the sound of the X5.

Esin turned and squinted through the rear window, clearly now sharing Balik's concern.

The approaching engines rose to a deafening roar. Three large trucks thronged past the BMW in the outside lane. Balik noticed the logos emblazoned on the side of the trucks and his eyes widened with recognition.

As though in military formation, the vehicles fanned out across the road in front of the BMW. Once diving side by side, the trucks slowed. Their brake lights made a chain of red across the asphalt. They slowed further, blocking the road ahead, forcing Balik to slow and then stop altogether.

31

———

Xanthe gripped the steering wheel as she pushed the Toyota to its limit. Streetlights streaked against the glass, their harsh glare casting eerie shadows across the roadway.

In the passenger seat, Leo peered at Ramiz, who was typing frantically on his laptop, his fingers a blur of motion. The glow of the screen illuminated his face, casting sharp shadows beneath his eyes and highlighting the tension in his jaw. It looked as though he was exchanging rapid-fire back-and-forth messages through an instant messenger system.

Remembering the confusing and convoluted explanation he'd received last time, Leo thought better of asking and settled back into his seat.

The towers of the Fatih Sultan Mehmet Bridge came into view. Leo sat up as he recognized the iconic structure from their journey up the Bosporus just a few hours ago.

"Come on," Ramiz whispered, his eyes flicking from the road to the screen and back again. "We're almost there."

Xanthe maneuvered the Toyota past a pair of cars and powered them out on the bridge. The road stretched out before them like a ribbon of asphalt suspended in midair. Leo glanced at the oily black water beneath them. The bridge's cables whipped past, shadows dancing across the road in a mesmerizing pattern of light and dark.

"Look! Look!" Ramiz shouted, pointing ahead. The brake lights of several vehicles flashed somewhere in the center of the bridge.

"Why is there a blockage at this time of night?" Leo asked.

Ramiz grinned.

Xanthe pulled into the other lane and flashed the Toyota's lights. A pair of cars shuffled out of the way.

Leo and Allissa strained upwards in their seats, attempting to see what was happening further down the road. To their right and left, the lights of Istanbul twinkled hypnotically on the surface of the water.

"Look at that!" Ramiz shouted, laughing out loud. He pointed at the laptop.

Leo leaned around the seat. The laptop showed a live news feed. A camera operator ran towards a stationary vehicle in the center of the multi-carriageway road. Leo recognized the cables and towers of the bridge in the background.

"There they are!" Xanthe said, swerving around another car. Two more cars blocked their way now. Xanthe slammed on the brakes and the Toyota squealed to a stop.

Xanthe and Ramiz piled out of the Toyota, quickly followed by Leo and Allissa. They charged past several cars already caught up in the blockage. Numerous drivers protested on their horns. Wind whipped across the carriage-way, almost pushing Leo into one of the waiting vehicles. Another impatient driver sounded the horn, the noise carried away by the strong crosswind.

Leo reached the front of the waiting cars and froze. Before them, in the middle of the carriageway, three news trucks blocked the road. And stopped before them, illuminated by floodlights attached to the news trucks and the headlights of the waiting cars, idled a BMW X5.

INSIDE THE BMW, Esin fumed. She looked from the approaching cameramen, to Balik, and then at Fasslane in the back.

She tried to swallow, but something felt as though it was stuck in her throat.

"What shall we do, boss?" Balik said. All the color drained from his face, too. His hands remained clamped to the steering wheel.

One of the camera operators approached Esin's window. The light attached to the camera shone into the car, washing everything in a ghostly glow. Esin covered her face with her hands—she still had a reputation to uphold and couldn't have them recognizing her.

The camera operator asked a question. Although Esin couldn't make out his words through the window she could guess what he was asking. She resisted the temptation to lower the glass and knock the camera to the ground.

Not getting the shot he wanted, the camera operator moved to the back of the X5. The light cut through the BWM's darkened windows, giving the camera operator a shot of Fasslane. Clearly excited, he shouted to the other camera operators, who quickly swarmed around the car.

"Boss?" Balik said, looking around. "We're completely blocked in here."

Esin peeked through her fingers toward the city center.

Two hundred feet below the roadway, the lights of a small boat bobbed and twinkled on the vast expanse of the Bosporus. She eyed Balik beside her, his bulky frame wedged into the driving seat, his scarred face set into a grimace.

As though out of the Bosporus itself, a plan began to form. Sure, this wasn't what they intended to happen, but the full story wasn't out yet. Maybe what they wanted was still achievable.

Headlines scrolled through Esin's mind. Quickly, in whispered Turkish, she explained her plan to Balik.

LEO WATCHED, rooted to the spot, as camera operators encircled the BMW X5. Bright lights from the waiting cars illuminated the scene. Car horns and irked shouts carried down the roadway as more vehicles joined the jam. The night wind whipped and sung through the bridge's suspension cables. Far below, the distant waters of the Bosporus lapped unseen.

Leo examined the news trucks for the first time. The vehicles bore the bold logos of their respective networks, standing out vividly under the harsh lights. Satellite dishes projected from the roofs, transmitting the scene live to the world. The trucks hummed with activity, their high-tech equipment broadcasting every detail of the unfolding events in real-time.

Ramiz stood between Leo and Allissa, his eyes wide, his body poised.

"How did—" Allissa pointed vaguely in the direction of the trucks.

"I've got a few trusted contacts in the industry," Ramiz

said. "I help them find the truth when they ask. But this is something else. This will make their careers."

One of the camera operators glanced at Ramiz and nodded. The operator then wheeled around to get a shot of the waiting traffic. The lens swept past Leo and Allissa. Leo resisted the temptation to duck out of shot.

At that moment, the driver's door of the X5 swung open and a burly man sprang out.

"Balik," Allissa whispered, recognizing the brute's scarred face.

Leo froze in position. Visions of the last time they'd seen the man passed through his memory at break-neck speed.

The camera operators wheeled around to frame Balik in the center of their shots.

Balik paced around the X5 and then yanked open the back door. He reached inside. The muscles in his arms strained as he attempted to pull something sizable from the backseat. His feet slipped across the roadway, before finding grip. His mouth twisted into a grim scowl. Balik pulled, but whatever was inside the car clearly didn't want to come out. For several seconds Balik strained, then finally hauled his quarry from the vehicle.

A man sprawled on the road. For a heartbeat he lay still, before clawing at the asphalt in an attempt to crawl away.

Unaware of the audience, Balik slammed the rear door of the X5, then turned calmly to face the other man.

"Brent Fasslane," Allissa whispered. "That's got to be Fasslane."

"But, what is he—" Leo muttered.

Balik strode over and lifted Fasslane from the road as though he weighed nothing. In the lights of the waiting cars, Leo saw that Fasslane's hair was now longer than on the videos and stubble scudded around his face.

Balik twisted Fasslane's arm to breaking point. Fasslane howled and bobbed up and down. Balik, his biceps bulging and his chin jutting forward, forced Fasslane up onto his tiptoes. Balik then turned away from the camera and shoved Fasslane across the road. Fasslane sprawled to the asphalt a few feet away. Balik paced across and was on him again in an instant. He lifted Fasslane up again and this time, half carried, half dragged him towards the edge of the bridge.

Clearly realizing his life was in danger, Fasslane suddenly lashed out, his fist connecting with Balik's jaw. Balik stumbled back, momentarily stunned by the unexpected blow. Fasslane seized the opportunity, wrenching himself free from Balik's grasp and staggered away.

Balik regained his footing and charged at Fasslane, his massive frame barreling toward him like a freight train. Fasslane swung around, his hands curling into fists.

The two men collided with a thud, their bodies slamming against each other in a tangle of limbs and fury. Fasslane drove his knee into Balik's gut, forcing the air from his lung. Balik grunted, but didn't slow, his hands clamped down on Fasslane's arms like vices.

Fasslane jerked his head forward, smashing his forehead against Balik's nose. Balik moved at the last moment, taking the blow on the cheek.

Balik roared with frustration and delivered a vicious kick to Fasslane's knee. Fasslane's leg buckled, and he dropped to one knee. Fasslane tried to stagger away, his chest heaving as he gulped in deep breaths of air. He glanced around wildly, clearly searching for an escape route, but there was nowhere to run.

Balik took the opportunity and lunged forward, his fists swinging in a flurry of blows. Fasslane ducked the first strike but wasn't quick enough for the second. Balik's giant fist smashed him in the mouth, causing blood to spurt forth.

Fasslane rocked forward and back as though he might collapse where he stood.

Balik seized Fasslane and dragged him toward the railing which flanked the edge of the bridge. Two hundred feet below on the other side of the railing, lay the open water of the Bosporus.

Balik's intention occurred to Leo like a punch to the gut. "He's going to throw him over!" he shouted.

The camera operators moved in silently, adjusting the lights mounted on top of their cameras to capture every part of the action.

Balik shoved Fasslane up against the railing. Muscles rippling, he held the smaller man tightly. Fasslane scraped and clawed at the Balik, attempting to pull himself away.

32

As though shaken from a trance, Leo, Allissa, and Ramiz rushed forward. Leo and Ramiz ran directly at Balik, their eyes locked on his muscular frame, silhouetted against the night sky.

Balik held Fasslane in both hands, his arms extended, his fingers digging into Fasslane's flesh. Fasslane kicked and struggled, his body thrashing in Balik's grasp like a fish caught on a hook. He swung an elbow, which struck Balik on the chin, but didn't even illicit a reaction.

Fasslane gurgled unintelligibly, his eyes wide with fear. He scratched at Balik's arms, leaving deep, bloody gouges. Balik didn't even notice.

Leo reached the railing. He peered over and then reeled back. The drop to the water beyond seemed to extend indefinitely, as though looking into a bottomless void. Leo seized Balik around the arms and attempted to yank the big man away from the edge.

Allissa looped her hands around Fasslane's waist, her face contorted with effort, she pulled with all her might.

Balik grimaced, his scarred grin widening, but no one

moved. Balik remained rooted to the spot. He held Fasslane in a vice-like grip.

Leo seized Balik around the neck. Tendons and veins bulged beneath Balik's skin, but the big man didn't yield. To Leo, it felt like clutching a tree trunk. Leo leaned back, attempting to topple the man on to the road and away from the perilous drop.

The wind howled harder. Leo's hair covered his face. Gusts thundered past his ears, rendering him unable to hear.

A moment later, the gusts subsided, and Leo heard a raised voice piercing through the chaos.

"Push!"

He recognized the voice instantly. It was Ramiz, his tone urgent and commanding.

Leo glanced at Ramiz, who stood beside them, his face inches from Leo's ear.

"Trust me," Ramiz said, his voice low and intense. "It's the only way. We push together."

Together, they stopped pulling Balik and Fasslane back towards the road and instead pushed them out into the void. Leo shoved Balik's broad back, his feet scrabbling for purchase on the slick concrete.

A flicker of confusion crossed Balik's face as he attempted to react to the sudden shift in direction. Bracing himself against pressure from one direction, he was unprepared for the change. His feet shuffled to correct his movement a moment too late. His massive frame teetered precariously on the edge of the bridge.

Leo and Allissa shoved harder, their hands slamming against Balik's shoulders. Ramiz threw his weight against Balik's back.

Balik staggered, his arms flailing as he fought to regain

his balance. In a state of panic, he let go of Fasslane, who crumpled to the ground, wheezing and panting.

The three shoved again, harder this time, their faces contorted with effort and determination.

Balik reached out desperately, his fingers clawing at the empty air. His body twisted and contorted as he fought against the inevitable.

With one final, mighty heave, Leo, Allissa, and Ramiz pushed with every ounce of strength they possessed. Balik's feet left the ground, his body arching backward over the void. His mouth opened in a silent scream of terror. Balik fell into the abyss, quickly swallowed by the darkness.

For a moment, there was only silence, broken by the ragged breathing and the distant roar of the traffic on the bridge. Then, as if released from a spell, Allissa rushed to Fasslane's side.

"What have we done?" Leo shouted, peering across the railing and into the void. Wind roared past his ears. Distant and indistinguishable water lapped two hundred feet below. Allissa and Ramiz joined him at the railing. All three studied the scene for several moments. Then, their expressions of worry merged into beaming smiles.

Twenty feet below, barely visible beyond the glare of the lights, Balik struggled and fought on the end of a cable. He hung upside down, swinging from side to side.

Leo followed the cable with his eyes. It was tied around Balik's ankles, looped up and over the railing and then around one of the bridge's suspansion cables.

Balik's voice drifted up to them as he struggled to right himself.

Leo shook his head slowly and then looked at Ramiz. "How did you... how did you think to do that?"

"It was pretty simple, really," Ramiz said, his hands on

his hips. "A simple balance of physical forces, calculations of weight, time, speed and density. Balik was clearly the heaviest, so trying to beat him on strength alone would be almost impossible, so I just—"

"Where's Xanthe?" Leo and Allissa interrupted in unison.

ESIN CLAMPED her hands across her face. She was determined that the news cameras wouldn't reveal her identity. She slid down in the seat and listened closely to the sound of movement and raised voices outside.

She counted the passing of another few seconds and then peeked through her fingers. At first, she saw the road ahead and the stationary news trucks. She twisted her head left and right, looking for the unwelcome, all-seeing lenses of the TV crews. Nothing. No one stood in front of the car. The TV trucks still blocked the road, but they appeared to be unmanned.

Esin lowered her hands and looked toward the edge of the bridge. She couldn't make out the action but could see that it had the attention of the surrounding cameras. Everyone was oblivious to her. Esin adjusted the X5's mirror and scanned the scene behind her. Several motorists had climbed from their cars and were watching the scene, too.

Then, in the mirror, she saw the distant blue flicker of emergency vehicles. Police, probably. It would take them some time to get there through the backed-up traffic, but they would get here eventually. Time was not on her side.

Esin glanced to the left. Cars on the opposite side of the carriageway, heading back to European Istanbul, crawled past. She saw one vehicle slow to a walking pace, desperate to see what disaster had caused such a delay.

"Sick," Esin muttered, grinning to herself.

She snapped open the glove box and searched through the contents, pulling things out onto the floor. The car's rental documents, a packet of mints, an empty box of cigarettes, a wad of fuel receipts. Her fingers touched something hard and cold at the back of the compartment.

"There you are," she said, sliding the gun beneath her belt.

Then, slowly and quietly, she popped open the door and stepped out onto the tarmac.

As RAMIZ, Allissa and Leo charged after Balik and Fasslane, Xanthe paused. She looked around. All eyes, including the camera crews, were focused on the brawling men. To Xanthe that all seemed a little too convenient. She didn't know for certain, but it would be unlike Esin Kartan to miss an event like this.

Xanthe crouched and scurried in behind one of the stationary cars just as the driver's door swung open and a man scrambled out to get a better look at the action. Xanthe moved around the car, keeping low until she was positioned behind the car's front wing. She peered out and surveyed the scene.

A flurry of shouts echoed from the far side of the bridge as the brawl continued. Xanthe resisted the temptation to look at whatever was happening there and remained focused on the BMW and the TV trucks, which still blocked the road.

A faint click issued from the BMW. Xanthe dropped out

of sight and peered beneath the cars. Slowly and silently, someone stepped out of the BMW, only visible by their shoes.

"Esin," Xanthe said, watching the movement closely.

Another flurry of shouts echoed from the fight at the edge of the bridge. Xanthe ignored it. Her eyes locked on the shoes as they took a tentative step away from the BMW.

Xanthe rose and tried to peer through the BMW, but the blacked-out glass made it almost impossible to see anything on the other side. She crouched down again and watched the shoes pace toward the median and the other lanes beyond.

Xanthe leaped to her feet and pounded across the tarmac. She reached the BMW in three strides and swung around the rear. Esin Kartan stood six feet away, her eyes fixed on the oncoming traffic.

Xanthe lunged forward, covering the distance in three large steps, and looped her arm around Esin's neck. Esin bent backward but remained on her feet. Xanthe pulled again, attempting to topple the other open over and restrain her on the ground. Esin's muscles tensed into coils of steel beneath her skin. She twisted around and seized Xanthe by the arm. With a grunt of effort, Esin dug her nails into Xanthe's skin and wrenched the arm away from her neck. Xanthe hissed in pain but didn't relent.

Esin shoved against the concrete median and slammed Xanthe into the side of the BMW. Xanthe loosened her grip for a moment but didn't yield.

Esin drove her elbow back, clearly aiming for Xanthe's ribs. Xanthe anticipated the move and spun to the side, using Esin's momentum to send her stumbling forward.

Esin caught herself on the hood of the car, her palms slapping against the metal. She whirled around and charged at Xanthe like a bull. Xanthe braced herself, her feet planted firmly on the ground, and met Esin's charge head-on.

They collided with a sickening thud, then Esin swung straight into a series of blows. Esin's fist slammed into Xanthe's jaw, snapping her head back and sending a jolt of white-hot pain through her skull. Xanthe tasted blood in her mouth, but she ignored it. She swung her own fist out, which caught Esin in the stomach.

Esin doubled over, the air rushing from her lungs in a whoosh. Xanthe seized the opportunity, tackling Esin to the ground and straddling her waist. With a roar of rage, Esin bucked her hips, throwing Xanthe off balance. In a flash, she reversed their positions, her hands wrapping around Xanthe's throat and squeezing with all her might.

Xanthe's eyes bulged as Esin's fingers dug, cutting off her air supply. She clawed desperately at Esin's hands, but the woman's grip was like iron. Black spots danced at the edges of Xanthe's vision as she struggled to breathe.

Before Xanthe knew what was happening, Esin dragged her across the median and into the oncoming traffic on the other side. The sound of blaring horns and screeching tires filled the air as they stumbled between vehicles.

With a last, desperate surge of energy, Xanthe brought her knee up, slamming it into Esin's stomach. Esin grunted in pain, her grip loosening for a split second. Xanthe wrenched herself free and stumbled backward.

Esin glanced at Xanthe, almost beaten on the side of the road, and then turned away. She removed a gun and leveled it at an oncoming car. The car screeched to a halt, fishtailing across the road.

Rage rose in Xanthe's throat. "There's no way you're getting away with this."

Xanthe spat gravel from her mouth, then charged

forward. With Esin facing the oncoming car, she covered the distance in a moment and then aimed two punches at Esin's stomach. The first one connected, knocking the older woman off balance.

Esin swung around, avoiding the second punch and attempting to bring the gun to bear.

The roadway shook as a giant truck rumbled past, sounding its horn. The sound of multiple sirens drifted down the roadway as several police cruisers weaved their way through the backed-up traffic.

"It's over," Xanthe shouted, holding her hands wide. "The police are here. Drop the gun or they'll shoot you where you're standing."

Esin snarled and glanced from the approaching blue lights to the road behind her, and then on to Xanthe. She retained her fighting stance.

Xanthe took another step backward, buying time.

Esin glanced behind her again. A car rumbled towards them in the middle lane, its headlights piercing through the night.

As the car approached, Esin stepped out into the middle of the lane, directly in the path of the oncoming vehicle. The driver slammed on the brakes and the car skidded to a halt.

Esin wasted no time. She yanked open the driver's side door, leveling her gun at the terrified motorist's head. "Out of the car, now!" she barked, her voice cold and commanding.

The driver, a middle-aged man in a suit, scrambled to comply, his hands shaking as he fumbled with his seatbelt. Esin grabbed him by the collar, hauling him out of the vehicle and shoving him to the ground.

Xanthe watched in horror as Esin turned her attention

back to her, a cruel smile playing across her lips. "Get in the car," she ordered, gesturing with the gun. "We're going for a ride."

Esin pulled the trigger, and a bullet smashed into the roadway just an inch from Xanthe's leg. "The next one's going through that pretty face of yours," Esin said. "Get in. You're driving."

33

____

Leo, Allissa and Ramiz searched the scene before them for signs of Xanthe. To their right, the TV trucks still sat blocking the traffic. To the left, cars waited for the blockage to pass, many motorists standing beside their vehicles. Police vehicles picked their way slowly through the congestion, lights strobing from the bridge's superstructure.

The BMW sat motionless, behind which the occasional car streamed towards the European side of the city. Then a car, its tires screeching, sped in the opposite direction.

Allissa, Leo and Ramiz dashed forward, swerved around the X5 and peered over the barrier. In the distance, a small yellow car powered down the inside lane.

"Xanthe," Ramiz said, breathless. "She must have been taken by... Esin."

A man stumbled into view from behind the BMW. His face was ashen, his eyes wide with shock and fear.

"That must be the driver of the car!" Ramiz said. "The one that Esin forced to stop!"

Leo and Allissa dragged the man across the barrier and

into the safety of the stationary traffic. He slumped down to the road, his body a dead weight.

"She... she had a gun," he stammered, his voice barely above a whisper. "Forced me out of the car. Took the woman... drove off..."

"She has an escape already planned out," Leo said, watching the taillights shrink to specks in the night. "She just didn't expect us to stop her here."

"Did she give you any indication of what they had planned?" Allissa asked Ramiz. "You said she was boasting about everything."

Ramiz shook his head. "Nothing. She just said they would be out of the city, and no one would find them."

"Can't we just trace the car?" Leo pointed at the ghostly shape, which was now almost invisible.

"How?" Ramiz said.

"You know, triangulate the immobilizer or something." Leo shrugged.

"No." Ramiz shook his head seriously.

"Hack the traffic cameras?" Allissa said hopefully.

"That'll take too long." Ramiz looked down at his feet. His shoulders slumped.

The whine of the sirens was almost upon them now. Leo turned to look at the approaching lights, shuffling through the blocked-up traffic. The voice of a police officer, berating a slow-moving motorist, carried through the air.

"I can help you." Leo, Allissa and Ramiz were startled by an American voice. They turned towards the sound.

"I know where they're going," Fasslane said, breathlessly. He staggered across the roadway and leaned against the fender of the BMW. He looked battered and bruised with a bloodied lip. He wiped the bedraggled hair from his eyes.

"Get me out of here before the cops arrive, and I'll show you."

"We need you to get this truck moved, now!" Ramiz shouted at one of the camera operators.

Recognizing Ramiz as the original source of their tip off, the man shouted at his colleague inside the truck. A few moments later, the engine coughed into life and the truck slid a few feet forward to allow them through.

Ramiz leaped into the passenger seat, and Allissa slid behind the wheel. Leo and Fasslane scrambled into the back. Allissa hit the ignition and the car's auto-start engaged. The key had never been removed.

With a flick of her wrist, Allissa shifted the automatic gearbox into drive, and the BMW shot forward. They rocketed past the TV trucks, the flashing lights of the police growing dimmer in the rearview mirror with each passing second.

"Start talking," Allissa said, eying Fasslane in the rearview mirror. "We've got you away from the police. Now tell us where Esin was going to take you."

Fasslane glanced up at her and then back down at his fingers.

"We're not wasting time," Leo said. "Talk now or we'll take you right back there to be exposed as the fraud you are."

"Esin has a place," Fasslane said. "It's a cabin in Uludağ."

"She said that no one knows about it," Fasslane continued. "It's off the record. Bought in a fake name or something, many years ago. She's got a car with fake places there. Totally clean, untraceable. We'd planned to spend a night there, maybe two, then I would head east. She had it all planned out."

"How far's the cabin?" Leo asked.

Ramiz leaned forward and poked at the sat nav system. Within seconds, he'd programmed the journey.

"It's just over 200km," he said, reading from the screen. "We'll be there in under three hours. Maybe nearer two if we don't hang around. Hold on a second, Uludağ." Concern clouded the young man's face.

"Yes, that's it. Up in the mountains somewhere," Fasslane said, shrugging. "I didn't even know you had mountains here."

"You know it?" Allissa turned to face Ramiz.

"No. Well, maybe." Ramiz looked at Allissa in wide-eyed shock. "I've only been there once. It was ten years ago. To see the place my father was killed in the car wreck."

34

The silence in the Renault Clio was only broken by Esin barking directions to Xanthe. As the car purred down the D575 freeway, Xanthe tried to figure out their destination. She knew they were heading south, so maybe Esin planned for them to go to Izmir, Usak, or on to Antalya itself.

Xanthe glanced at Esin in the passenger seat, the gun cradled in her lap.

"Slow down," Esin said as they approached the town of Bursa. "We don't want to draw attention to ourselves."

Rolling through the town, Xanthe looked around at the squat concrete buildings. Most lay in darkness, the residents still hours away from rising. A few twinkled with the lights of early activity.

In the distance, against the star-studded sky, Xanthe got her fight sight of Uludağ's brooding figure. The mountain soared above the town, as though threatening to blot out the sky altogether. A chime of something akin to realization appeared in her mind. She focused in on it, tried to make sense of it.

Xanthe played with the thought as Esin reeled off the

directions through the town and out onto a mountain road. The buildings thinned out again as they climbed the winding road. The little car whined and struggled up the incline. The road twisted skywards, frost now hanging on branches which reached out across the sky. Through the occasional break in the trees, Xanthe saw the lights of Bursa growing small beneath them. With the altitude, the weather closed in too.

"It's funny, even after all these years, this road reminds me of your father," Esin said.

Xanthe glanced at her. The older woman toyed with the gun, smiling.

"You don't remember, do you? Oh bless," Esin said.

Realization pinned Xanthe to the seat, pushing her shoulders back into the worn-out padding.

"There we are," Esin said, watching Xanthe's expression turn to stone. "The moment of realization can be a beautiful thing."

"Our father died on this road," Xanthe whispered, glancing from the road ahead to Esin.

"Correct," Esin said.

"You?" Xanthe hissed between gritted teeth.

Esin cackled, slapping her thigh with amusement. "I think your father overestimated his dear children. Imagine you two, in charge of a billion-lira business! Ha!"

"Why?" Xanthe said in astonishment. "No wait, I know. You wanted the business when he retired, and he wouldn't give it to you."

"Correct," Esin said, nodding.

At that moment, light and the thronging of a powerful engine filled the Renault. Xanthe glanced in the mirror to see bright headlights sweeping up the road behind them.

ALLISSA DROVE through the empty streets quickly. She had to admit, the X5 was a great vehicle to drive. It had the power to cruise at high speeds, without reducing comfort. It was the opposite of the rust bucket Leo had bought and then sold a few months ago. On the entire two-and-a-half-hour journey, only a few words were spoken in the car. The four wore expressions of fatigue and anxiety.

Allissa powered out of the town of Bursa and on to the slender road leading up towards Uludağ. Trees flanked the road on both sides. Allissa glanced up at the mountain. Snow covered the high banks of the imposing slopes. She slid down the window, letting a cool breeze whip into the car.

Allissa gripped the wheel tightly as she powered the car around a sharp corner, the thick tires sliding for a heart-stopping moment before finding their grip and sending a cloud of gravel pinging into the barrier. She eased off the accelerator, applying the brake gently to slow their speed. Losing control on a road like this could be fatal, and she was all too aware of the steep drop-off that loomed just inches from the edge of the pavement.

The X5 rounded the corner, revealing a new curve of tarmac that led up and around the mountain slope in a dizzying spiral. Allissa scanned the road ahead, her senses on high alert for any sign of the car they were chasing.

Ramiz shot forward in the passenger seat, his small frame suddenly alert and energized. "There, look!" he shouted, pointing frantically through the windshield.

"What?" Allissa said, her gaze darting from the road to Ramiz and back again. She had been so focused on navigating the perilous corner that she had missed whatever it was that Ramiz had seen.

Behind them, Leo and Fasslane sat forward. They had been dozing in the backseat, but now they were fully awake, their minds focused on the task at hand.

"There was a car. I'm sure of it," Ramiz insisted, his finger shaking with excitement. "The rear lights just disappeared around the next corner."

Allissa squinted, seeing nothing but the endless expanse of the mountain road ahead. "There's only one way to find out," she said, clicking the BMW into manual transmission and gripping the wheel with renewed vigor.

The engine roared, and the BMW surged forward. They covered the straight section in mere seconds, tires cutting a pair of tracks through the ice-crusted tarmac.

As they approached the next corner, Allissa dropped a gear. The engine growled hungrily. The rev counter strobed into the red, but the car stayed on course, swinging around the bend in a screeching blur of motion. Grit and snow flew into the air, obscuring their vision for a moment before settling back onto the road.

"There. There!" Ramiz yelled as the next curve of the mountain road appeared ahead of them, glowing silver in the moonlight. A few hundred feet ahead a small yellow car strained up the mountain road, its taillights glowing red.

"That's them, I'm sure of it!" Ramiz exclaimed, his voice shaking.

Allissa glanced at him, her brow furrowed with concern. "How sure? We only saw them at a distance."

"Sure. Totally sure," Ramiz said.

Allissa hit the gas once more. The engine's growl turned into a roar as they surged up the incline. She moved through the gears, accelerating on a short straight section of the road. They reached the next corner. Allissa feathered the brakes and sent the BMW into a controlled slid. The tires screeched as they fought for grip on the icy road. The car shuddered and swayed, but she kept it under control. They rounded the bend, and the yellow car came back into view.

"We're gaining ground," Allissa said, once again down-shifting.

The yellow car swerved and skidded around the next corner, its tires struggling to find purchase on the icy road. Allissa's eyes narrowed as she saw the car fishtail, the rear end swinging out precariously close to the edge of the cliff.

"They're losing control," she muttered, her hands tightening on the wheel.

"Be careful," Ramiz said, leaning forward. "If you go over the edge here." He pointed at the barrier, beyond which lay a drop of several hundred feet.

Allissa nodded, her jaw clenched with determination. The next corner approached fast. Allissa saw the lights of another vehicle approaching. She hit the brake, sending them all jarring into their seat belts. She swung the wheel and pulled them into the lane behind the yellow car. An old Land Rover rumbled around the corner, passing them by inches.

"We've got to stop them," Fasslane said, his voice weak. "If Esin gets to her cabin with the new vehicle, she'll be untraceable."

Allissa thumped the accelerator again. The BMW gained on the small car easily. Allissa pulled out again into the other lane. She was just about to overtake when the yellow car broke heavily. Red lights filled the BMW. Allissa squinted and stamped on the brake.

An almighty crunch vibrated through the BMW, followed by the sound of shattering glass.

35

———————

Esin's voice cut through the roar of the engine, her eyes blazing with a frantic intensity. "Faster! We have to lose them now!"

Xanthe gripped the steering wheel tighter. She squinted against the blinding glare of the headlights in the rearview mirror. The powerful car behind them was closing in, its menacing presence growing larger with each passing second. In a heart-stopping moment, their pursuer swerved out to attempt an overtake, the sound of screeching tires barreling up the mountain.

A flicker of a smile played at the corners of Xanthe's lips. Though she had yet to lay eyes on the occupants of the car, there was no doubt in her mind who was behind the wheel. With a calculated move, she eased off the accelerator, allowing the Renault to slow just enough. The engine of the other car roared as it pulled alongside, just inches separating the two vehicles as they hurtled along the winding mountain road.

Esin jabbed the cold barrel of the gun into Xanthe's ribs.

"I said faster! Don't test me. This gun isn't for show. If you're not going to drive properly, you're no use to me."

Xanthe reluctantly gave the Renault some gas, propelling them in front of the other vehicle. The blinding glare of oncoming headlights pierced the night, forcing their pursuers to swerve back into position behind them.

Xanthe risked a glance at Esin. The harsh, angular features of the older woman were illuminated by the ghostly glow of the dashboard lights as she whipped around in the passenger seat. Her eyes, wide and wild, locked onto the vehicle charging back up behind them, its powerful engine roaring as it quickly regained the ground it had lost. The gun hung loose in Esin's grasp.

While Esin's focus was elsewhere, Xanthe slammed her foot on the brake pedal. The Renault fishtailed, its tires gouging out jagged streaks of ice and gravel as they fought for purchase. The tires found their grip, and the Renault screamed to a stop.

The BMW slammed into the back of the Renault. Metal crumpled like paper. The Renault's rear end folded in on itself, the rear window exploding in a shower of glass. The Renault shot across the road, skidding sideways as if it were nothing more than a toy.

Inside the smaller car, Esin's body shot forward. Not wearing her seatbelt, her head smashed into the dashboard with a nauseating crack.

A blinding light flooded the interior of the small car.

Her ears screaming, Xanthe spun around in her seat. She lashed out and slapped the gun from Esin's grasp, sending it clattering into the rear footwell.

Esin, recovering with a surprising swiftness, lunged at Xanthe, her fingers outstretched like the claws of a predatory cat. Xanthe tried to move backward, but her reaction came a fraction of a second too late. Esin's nails raked across her face, leaving a searing trail of blood.

Gritting her teeth against the agony, Xanthe retaliated with a sharp elbow to Esin's jaw, followed by a powerful blow to her stomach. Esin doubled over, gasping for air.

Xanthe seized the opportunity. With fumbling fingers, she undid her seatbelt and shoved open the door.

Esin howled, a mix of rage and desperation as she made a frantic grab for Xanthe's arm. Xanthe leaned back and lashed out once more, her fist connecting with Esin's temple. Then Xanthe gathered her remaining strength and sprang out of the car.

Seeing Xanthe stagger from the Renault, Leo and Ramiz scrambled out of the BMW and ran to help. They raced towards her, their feet pounding against ice-covered asphalt.

One of the BMW's lights had been smashed in the collision, but the remaining one cast a strange angular light across the scene. Shadows and reflections bounced from the Renault's splintered rear.

Xanthe stumbled down the road towards her brother and Leo. Her steps were unsteady, her body swaying as if dragged by an invisible force. The adrenaline that had fueled her escape was now clearly giving way to exhaustion.

Ramiz charged up and embraced his sister. Xanthe melted into his grip, her body shaking.

"Esin has a gun," Xanthe said between ragged breaths, her voice barely above a whisper. She pointed a trembling finger towards the Renault.

Leo froze in his position. The Renault was just a few strides away. Something moved in the car's shadowy interior. He took another step towards the crumpled car, and then two more.

"Leo, be careful!" Xanthe shouted.

The Renault's engine whined gently.

Leo reached the rear of the car. He bent down and peered through the shattered rear windscreen.

Esin moved and then groaned. In the strange half-light from the BMW's single headlight, he couldn't see Esin clearly.

"Step out of the car now," Leo shouted, forcing confidence into his voice. "The police will be here very soon."

The noise which came from the car sounded more animal than human.

Steeling himself, Leo strode around to the open driver's door. Just inside the door, he could see the keys dangling from the ignition block. He reached forward, aiming to remove the keys.

The door slammed shut before he reached it. He glanced up and saw Esin drag herself into the driver's seat. The woman sneered at him and then revved the engine.

"Wait, wait!" Leo shouted, scrambling for the door handle.

The tires spun, flinging dust, glass and shards of broken metal into the air.

Leo grabbed the handle just as the car pulled away, the front swinging violently up the road.

"Get in, now!" Allissa yelled, her voice cutting through the frigid night air as she revved the BMW.

Xanthe and Ramiz piled into the back seat. Leo leapt into the passenger seat. The doors slammed, and Allissa wasted no time in pulling away.

Ahead of them, the Renault sped up the winding mountain road, its battered frame cutting two deep, twisting tracks into the freshly laid snow.

Allissa squinted into the darkness, her eyes locked onto the Renault's single working taillight. The silvery glow of the moon cast an ethereal light across the snow-capped peaks. It was clear that Esin was pushing the car to its limits, the engine straining against the steep incline and the treacherous conditions.

As the road curved sharply to the left, Leo leaned forward in his seat, his gaze fixed on the Renault's taillights. He watched intently, expecting to see the telltale flicker of brake lights as Esin navigated the treacherous turn. But none came. Instead, the Renault continued to accelerate, hurtling towards the corner with a reckless abandon.

"The corner," Leo said urgently. He pointed towards the rapidly approaching bend. "She's going way too fast for the corner."

The snow-covered guardrail was only just visible in the moonlight, a flimsy barrier that seemed wholly inadequate in the face of the impending disaster. The Renault's tires kicked up a spray of snow and gravel as it neared the turn, its headlights cutting through the darkness.

36

Esin pushed the pedal to the floor as the small car climbed the icy road. The wheels, which had spun and fishtailed to the right and left, had now found a steady forward motion.

She studied the road ahead. She was now just a couple of miles from the cabin. Just a little closer and she could make it on foot. Cutting through the forest further up the slope, she could use the tree cover to obscure her tracks. They would be so close, but impossibly far too. If she could just get out of sight, she would make a dash for it.

Esin glanced in the mirror. The BMW had started up the slope behind her. Whilst it was a vastly more suitable vehicle, the driver didn't know where they were going. Esin, on the other hand, had been driving these roads for decades. She knew every rise and fall, every twist and turn.

Approaching the corner, Esin gave the little car more gas. The engine's hum became a whine. Tires grunted and sloshed through the snow, struggling for traction.

Esin swung the wheel hard to the left. Through the windscreen the crash barrier, protecting traffic from a perilous drop, loomed ever closer.

"Come on, come on," she whispered.

Tires groaned, kicking snow and dirt in great arcs on either side of the car. The Renault swung to the left and then to the right. The barrier drifted closer. The thin metal strip filled the windscreen, beyond which, the featureless night sky stretched out into nothing. The Renault rumbled and shook. Then, by some miracle, the tires hit solid ground. The Renault swerved to the left, dirt and gravel spraying up all around.

The change in direction swung her to the side. The headlights swept from the road ahead, out into the void, and back again. The car flew on, bouncing from one side of the road to the other.

Esin glanced in the mirror and then at the next corner, which lay a few hundred feet ahead. If she could just get there, then she would be home and dry. She straightened out the wheel and steeled her expression. Then, as though in slow motion, the car slipped to the left.

THE OCCUPANTS of the BMW watched in silent horror as the Renault spun out of control. A sickening ballet of rubber and ice played out against the backdrop of the mountains. Tire marks crisscrossed the road. Snow and ice sprayed up in all directions, glittering in the moonlight like a cascading veil of diamonds. The car spun twice, its momentum carrying it towards the edge of the mountain road, where no barrier stood between the vehicle and the perilous drop.

In the murky depths far below, icy trees shivered, their branches reaching up like skeletal fingers.

Allissa carefully increased the BMW's speed. The engine purred, inching them closer to the stricken vehicle.

The Renault's wheels locked as Esin attempted frantically to stop. The car continued its reverse slide towards the precipice. Tires rattled through the compacted snow, the sound like the chatter of a thousand teeth. The rear of the Renault slid clear of the abyss, teetering on the brink.

Time seemed to stretch, each second an eternity as the Renault slowed but continued its relentless drift backward. The car dropped onto its chassis with a crunch. A stream of rock and ice skipped down the mountain, disappearing amid the trees. The Renault rocked backward. The chassis groaned as it scraped against the road's edge.

The occupants of the BMW watched in silence as the Renault teetered one way and then the other.

Allissa hit the brake, and the X5 slid to a stop a few feet from the Renault. The X5's single beam washed the scene in cool bright light. The Renault swung gently from nose to tail, teetering on the edge. In the driver's seat, Esin gripped the wheel. She wore a strange expression of determination.

Leo and Allissa leaped out of the BMW and ran towards the Renault. Ramiz, Xanthe and Fasslane followed.

Leo reached the front of the Renault and took hold of the front bumper. He heaved as hard as he could, but the car wouldn't move. Allissa joined him and together they pulled, hoping that an inch of movement would secure the car on the roadway.

"No!" Xanthe said, rushing up beside them. "Let go of that now!"

"What?" Leo said, turning to look at Xanthe.

"This woman killed our father, right here on this road!" She doesn't deserve to be saved. Xanthe leapt at the hood of the car, shoving it further toward the precipice.

"No! Don't!" Allissa shouted. "We've got too—"

Leo tried to grab the front bumper, but Ramiz seized

him. The small man held him back as his Xanthe shoved at the bumper again.

Esin released the clutch and the front wheels spun, the rubber clawing at the slick road in a vain attempt to pull the car back to safety. Snow and grit flew into the air, forcing Leo and Allissa to turn away.

Xanthe pushed, shoving the front bumper with all the strength she could muster. The car groaned, its metal frame screaming in agony as it scraped against the asphalt.

Xanthe's feet dug into the road and the Renault rocked backward. The wheels spun pointlessly an inch above the road. Xanthe shoved again, her muscles tensing with the pent-up pain of loss and deceit.

Then, finally, gravity took over. The engine noise died, replaced by the sickening sound of grinding and scraping.

The car slid freely for a few heart-stopping moments, suspended in a void between earth and sky, before crashing into the unforgiving slope of the mountain. The sound of shattering glass pierced the night air, accompanied by the explosive pop of a tire.

More glass shattered. The Renault flipped over and smashed onto its roof. It scraped upside down across the jagged rocks for a few seconds before flipping again.

Leo and Allissa stepped up beside Xanthe. The Renault continued its relentless descent, bumping and crashing through the darkness, its headlights casting erratic beams of light that danced and flickered. The car's progress was marked by the trail of debris it left in its wake—shards of glass, twisted metal, and other scattered remnants.

As the wind whipped around them, Leo inhaled a deep lungful of the crisp mountain air, the cold burning his lungs and sharpening his senses. He intertwined his fingers with Allissa's.

"We can't save everyone," he said, his voice barely audible above the howling wind.

"Not everyone deserves saving," Allissa replied, looking from Xanthe and on to Ramiz.

37

Dawn broke slowly across the slopes of Uludağ. First, the sky lightened to a deep indigo, muting the swathes of stars into a stubborn few that clung to the heavens. Then a stripe of fiery orange rose from the horizon, consuming more stars in its wake. Finally, sometime later, creamy sunlight streamed across the snow-covered landscape, washing out the remaining stars altogether.

Leo and Allissa stood on the front porch of Esin's cabin and looked out at the spectacular display unfolding before them. The air was crisp and cold, their breath misting in front of their faces. Leo put his arm around Allissa's waist and pulled her in close, savoring her warmth against the morning chill.

"It's a beautiful place," Leo said, looking at the rustic wood cabin nestled among the frost-covered pines. Icicles hung in long fingers from the eaves, glinting in the pale sunlight.

"Yeah, it is. A perfect place to hide from evil crimes, right?" Allissa replied. The golden light of dawn reflected in her eyes.

"Maybe we should get a place like this and forget about the city altogether. What do you think?" Leo said.

Allissa looked out at the majestic, snow-capped peaks on the horizon. "With the nearest shop over ten miles away? No chance. I've always preferred cities, anyway."

Leo glanced down at the BMW X5 parked at the end of the track below them, recalling the arduous drive up the winding mountain roads. It had taken them almost an hour, using Fasslane's scant directions, to find the secluded cabin.

"Something tells me you enjoyed driving that thing, though?" Leo said, pointing at the car with a grin.

"Yes, it's a nice car," Allissa admitted. Leo opened his mouth to speak again, but Allissa cut him off. "And absolutely no to your next question."

"But—" Leo protested playfully.

"Guys, I think we're ready," Xanthe interrupted, appearing at the cabin's front door.

The interior of the cabin was warm and welcoming, a stark contrast to the frigid wilderness outside. A crackling fire burned in the stone hearth, filling the room with its cozy glow and the comforting scent of wood smoke. Steaming mugs of coffee sat on the table, wisps of steam curling lazily into the air.

"Esin had thought of everything here," Xanthe said, directing Leo and Allissa towards the coffee. "There's enough food and fuel for a couple of weeks, at least."

"Are you sure I have to do this?" Fasslane said, his voice tinged with anguish. He sat slumped in an armchair, his face haggard and his eyes haunted.

Allissa, Xanthe, and Leo turned to face him. Ramiz stood in the far corner, holding a smartphone.

"You have two options," Allissa replied firmly. "You do

this now, or you take your chances with the police. Your lies have caused a lot of trouble in the last few weeks."

"I do this and then I can disappear?" Fasslane asked, a note of desperate hope in his voice.

The four exchanged glances. Each knew that the real villain had already faced a grim form of justice. Their quarrel wasn't with this broken man before them.

"Yes," Leo said. "We will leave you here. You can stay or go as you please."

Fasslane nodded grimly and then looked down at his hands, as if seeing the weight of his misdeeds reflected there.

"Ready?" Ramiz asked, checking the camera settings on the phone.

Fasslane nodded again. He straightened up in the chair and took a deep breath.

Ramiz gave a thumbs up, signaling that the camera was rolling.

Allissa and Leo glanced at each other and then each took a long sip of the hot coffee.

Fasslane looked directly into the camera lens, his eyes sorrowful but determined. He began to speak, his voice heavy with remorse.

"My name is Brent Fasslane. I'm recording this video to confess that the claims I made in my book, *A New World Order*, were false. I knowingly spread misinformation and stoked people's worst fears for my own selfish gain."

He paused, swallowing hard. His hands trembled in his lap.

"I am deeply sorry for the harm I have caused. The chaos, the unrest, the damaged relationships between nations - it's all because of my lies. I wanted fame and notoriety so badly that I was willing to deceive the entire world to get it."

"I realize now how wrong I was. My ego and greed blinded me to the suffering I was causing. I exploited people's distrust in their leaders and institutions for my benefit. It was inexcusable."

Fasslane took a shuddering breath.

Watching his admission, Leo had to admit the guy was either genuine or a good actor.

"I know I can never fully undo the damage I've done," Fasslane continued. "But I'm making this video to take responsibility, to admit that I lied, and to urge everyone I misled to reject the poisonous fantasies I peddled."

Fasslane looked imploringly at the camera. "Please, don't let my selfishness and deceit divide us any further. The world faces real challenges that we must confront together, with clear eyes and open hearts. I'm so profoundly sorry for pulling us apart with my lies."

He straightened up, his jaw tight with resolve. "I will step out of the public eye now and strive to make amends however I can, quietly and humbly. I only hope that my confession today helps heal some of the wounds I've inflicted on our society."

Fasslane nodded solemnly to the camera, signaling the end of his speech. Silence descended over the room, broken only by the pop and hiss of the logs in the fireplace.

<h1 style="text-align:center">38</h1>

<hr>

Brighton, England. A week later.

The afternoon sun cast a warm glow through the window of Leo and Allissa's apartment. Boxes were piled against the wall of the room, overflowing with books, DVDs, and an eclectic mix of mementos from their adventures together.

Leo swept up a pair of books and dropped them into a box as the doorbell buzzed.

"Are we expecting anyone?" Allissa said, glancing toward the door.

"Not that I know of." Leo placed the box on the table and lumbered across to the door. He tried the intercom system, but it didn't work as usual. He wandered down the stairs, returning a minute later with Marcus Green in tow.

"I don't know how you did it," Green said, bounding into the room and pointing a finger first at Leo, then Allissa. "But you did it. It was incredible. Absolutely incredible. I can't believe you got a video from the man himself confessing that it was all a figment of his twisted imagination. Amazing. I thought you'd come up with some solid evidence, or a money trail, not a personal confession. Where is Fasslane now?"

"He's gone underground," Leo replied, placing a pair of well-worn travel guides into the box. "And I don't expect we'll be seeing him for some time. Probably for the best, all things considered."

"Well, I suppose that doesn't really matter now," Green said, shaking his head in amazement. If he'd noticed the state of disarray the house was in, he didn't mention it. "But wow, just wow. I owe you big time for this. Fasslane's confession has been the most watched video on the planet. This is big. Monumental. It changes everything."

"You gave us the initial info," Allissa said. She glanced at Leo, smiling. "As usual, we just followed the rabbit hole to its end."

"You did a fantastic job of it, I can tell you that," Green said. "But I'm here to give you another opportunity, actually. This could make you some serious money. I'm talking thousands. All I'd need is an on-record interview with you about what you did and how it all came together. A blow-by-blow account of your investigation."

Leo and Allissa glanced at each other, a flicker of amusement passing between them.

"We could tell you," Leo said slowly, walking to the front door and holding it open in a pointed gesture. "But you would never believe us. Some stories are just too wild for print."

"Okay, okay, I get it." Green held up his hands in mock surrender. "But seriously, you name your fee. This is, quite literally, the biggest story in the world right now. Whatever you want, I can get it for you. Just think about it."

"See you later, Marcus," Allissa called over her shoulder, dropping a stack of magazines into another box.

Green turned to face Leo, his expression almost pleading. "Come on, you've got to give me something. Name your price. An exclusive tell-all would absolutely blow up. It could make your careers!"

"Thanks for dropping in, but we really must get on," Leo said, nodding towards the door.

Green shook his head and paced toward the exit. On the threshold, he turned back, his gaze flickering between Leo and Allissa.

"You know, there's always been something special about you two," he said. "I don't understand it one bit." He fished in his jacket pocket and handed Leo a business card. "If you do change your mind, give me a call, anytime. Day or night. I mean it."

Marcus Green turned and disappeared down the narrow staircase.

Another week later.

"I'm going to miss this place," Allissa said wistfully, her voice barely audible over the din of the pub as she led Leo out through the heavy wooden doors. The familiar scent of ale and the sound of laughter faded behind them, replaced by the crisp evening air.

"We'll come back, I'm sure," Leo replied, trying to sound reassuring as he joined her on the cobblestone street.

Leo pulled his coat tightly around himself, shivering as the cold wind whipped in from the sea. Allissa looped her scarf around her neck once more. The vibrant hues of the leaves swirling around their feet were a stark reminder that winter was coming.

"We're not going to come all the way out here from our new place, though, are we?" Allissa said.

"If we were to live in that place we saw today, I don't think we'd ever have to leave. You know, with the sea views *and* integrated appliances," Leo said, attempting to lighten the mood by mimicking the overly enthusiastic voice of the real estate agent who had shown them the apartment.

"You better not mean that," Allissa warned, digging him in the ribs. "I'm not becoming one of those people who just stays in all the time, staring at the same four walls. You'll miss this place too, right? You've been here longer than me."

They reached the corner and the Victorian building that housed their apartment came into view. Leo felt a sudden tightness in his chest as he gazed up at their window on the top floor. The apartment looked dark and forlorn. The wind barreled around the corner with a newfound ferocity, causing Leo to shudder.

He stood there for a long moment, unable to tear his eyes away from the building that had been his home for so long. Memories flooded his mind—late nights spent poring over case files, lazy Sunday mornings, laughter-filled evenings with friends.

Beside him, Allissa slipped her hand into his, her fingers icy against his skin.

"There's something I need to tell you," Leo said.

"Can't it wait until we get inside? It's cold." Allissa shivered dramatically.

"No," Leo said, rooted to the spot. "Can you see anything different?" Leo pointed up at their building.

Allissa sighed, her breath forming a delicate mist. Reluctantly, she turned to face the building, her eyes tracing the weathered bricks.

"No, I don't think—let's just get—" she began.

"Look closely," Leo said, encircling Allissa with his arms.

Allissa's brow furrowed in confusion, her gaze sweeping over the building. And then, with a sudden jolt of realization, she saw it. Or rather, she saw what was missing.

"Wait, the *for sale* sign. It's gone!" she said. She spun around in Leo's arms, searching his face for an explanation. "What... I don't understand."

"Well, earlier today I made a phone call and, I, well..." He paused, taking a deep breath before continuing. "I bought the apartment... we bought the apartment."

Allissa's jaw dropped, her mind reeling as she tried to process his words.

"You can't have," she said, her voice barely above a whisper. She folded her arms across her chest. "I don't understand. We had nowhere near enough money even for the down payment."

Leo's gaze dropped to the ground, his cheeks flushing with a hint of shame. "Yeah, well... I did the interview with Green. He paid enough for a generous down payment on the place, and the monthly payments are almost the same as we were paying, anyway." He shifted his weight from foot to foot. "Come on, let's get inside. It's freezing."

Allissa stood immobile for a moment, her mind spinning with a thousand questions. Then, snapping her jaw shut with an audible click, she hurried after him.

"Wait, wait, wait!" Allissa said, chasing Leo inside. She caught up to him on the stairs. "What did you tell Green?"

Leo paused on the landing, his hand resting on the banister. "Well, I might have made a few things up," he said. "In fact, he sent me a copy of the article earlier. I'll let you read it. But more important than that... welcome home."

Unraveling the Lies: An Exclusive Interview with Leo Keane, the Investigator Who Exposed Brent Fasslane

By Marcus Green

BRIGHTON - In a cozy pub nestled in the heart of Brighton, I sit across from Leo Keane, one half of the investigative duo responsible for unmasking the deception behind Brent Fasslane's global scandal. With a disarming grin, Keane shrugs off the magnitude of his achievement. "It was nothing, really," he says, taking a sip of his drink. "We were just in the right place at the right time."

I remind him that the Fasslane affair had far-reaching consequences, souring relationships between world powers, sparking protests in the streets, and humiliating numerous high-profile figures. Keane's grin widens as he leans back in his chair. "You're right," he concedes. "But it wasn't as difficult as you might think. We've been doing this sort of thing for a while now."

Indeed, Keane and his partner, Allissa Stockwell, have made a name for themselves as expert investigators. They first shot to prominence during the highly publicized trial of Stockwell's father, Blake Stockwell, and have since successfully tracked down several missing persons across the globe.

Keane attributes their success to a keen eye for detail. "People think they can just move on to another place without leaving a trace, but that's not true," he explains. "Wherever you go, there are clues to your next intention and indications of where you've been. As investigators, we're finely tuned to notice these things."

He gestures around the pub. "Take this place, for example. We're not bothering anyone here, but I bet at least ten people could vouch for our presence, and there are multiple cameras recording us."

The conversation turns to the crux of the matter: how Keane and Stockwell managed to locate Brent Fasslane when the rest of the world was left in the dark. Keane leans forward, a conspiratorial glint in his eye.

"The big break came when we tracked down a maid who had been working at Fasslane's hotel in Istanbul. It's amazing what people notice if it's unusual. She'd been cleaning his room one day and noticed a lot of cold weather clothing in his suitcase." This observation, apparently, led Keane and Stockwell to conclude that Fasslane's next move would be to a colder location.

"All we had to do was look for nearby places with cooler temperatures at that time of year. Uludağ was our first thought. It's just a few hours away by car and doesn't cross any international borders. We traveled out there and spent an afternoon asking people if a lone American man had been staying on the mountain. We got lucky again. Right place, right time."

I press Keane on the reported incident on the Fatih Sultan Mehmet Bridge and the rumors of involvement by an underground group called the *Guardians of Truth*. At this, Keane laughs, shaking his head.

"Now you're the one making things up, Marcus. Haven't you learned anything from reading Fasslane's book?"

A dream proposal turns into a heart-stopping nightmare when Leo's fiancée vanishes without a trace in the tropical paradise of Koh Tao.

Travelling the world with the love of his life, Leo's looking for the perfect place to propose. Reaching the Thai tropical paradise of Koh Tao, he thinks he's found it.

But before he gets an answer, she's nowhere to be seen.

On searching the resort, his tranquillity turns to turmoil. What began as a dream escape swiftly spirals into a harrowing quest as he must to work out whether this is a practical joke gone wrong, or something much more sinister.

Discover where it all began in KOH TAO BETRAYAL, the compelling introduction to Luke Richardson's Best-selling International Detective Series.

Grab your FREE copy now!
www.lukerichardsonauthor.com/kohtao

AUTHOR'S NOTE

Although not based on any particular living character, I think we all know a Brent Fasslane! Turn on any news channel and you don't have to wait long to see one—sometimes they are politicians, other times criminals, but they always put their frivolous wants in front of anyone else's. It's great fun to write characters like this, but less fun to actually spend time with them.

By the way, Brent Fasslane returns in my book, the Atlantis Agenda... and yes, he is creating more trouble on a global scale (some people never learn).

Check out The Atlantis Agenda here: www.lukerichard sonauthor.com/atlantis

I originally visited Istanbul in 2016, which is the trip that inspired this book. One thing that stood out to me on that trip, and isn't featured in this book, is the train station which used to be the terminal for the Orient Express. It's a wonderful piece of architecture and speaks of a time when traveling across land was the only option. That gave me an idea, and seven years later I set out on my own train journey, with the target of reaching Istanbul all over land. Ten countries and four weeks later, I arrived to meet my friend and fellow thriller author Steven Moore. It was great to show him around some of the city's highlights including those mentioned in this story.

The cisterns of Istanbul are a true marvel, a testament to the ingenuity of the ancient Romans and Byzantines. The most famous amongst them is the Basilica Cistern, also known as the Sunken Palace. Comprising of 336 columns arranged in 12 rows, you can't help but feel a sense of awe at the scale and beauty of this ancient water storage system. The city is home to a vast network of these underground water storage facilities, built over the course of centuries to ensure a reliable water supply for the city's growing population.

The cisterns come in various sizes and styles, from small, simple chambers to large, ornate underground halls. Some, like the Basilica Cistern, are open to the public and have become popular tourist attractions, while others remain hidden and largely unknown.

In recent years, as Istanbul has undergone rapid development and construction, new cisterns have been discovered beneath the city's streets and buildings. In 2014, for example, a massive cistern dating back to the Byzantine era was discovered during the construction of a hotel in the city's Sultanahmet district. The cistern, which measures 138 feet long and 115 feet wide, is believed to have been built in the 6th century AD and was likely used to store water for the Great Palace of Constantinople. Learning about this gave me the idea for Ramiz's secret hide out, and the dramatic scenes that play out there.

Hagia Sophia, once a church, then a museum and now a mosque, is another of Istanbul's most iconic landmarks. The building's soaring dome and intricate mosaics are a testament to the skill and artistry of the Byzantine architects who created it. Standing beneath the dome, you can't help but look skyward and imagine the prayers and hymns that have filled the space for over 1,500 years.

Istanbul's unique position at the crossroads of Europe and Asia is perhaps best exemplified by the Bosporus Strait, which divides the city into its European and Asian sides.

As it stands, this is the final book in this series, and for me is something of a closure. This series has so far marked over five years of my life.

In the last few days of 2017, I started writing the story which would be Kathmandu in a café in Madrid, Spain. I was there visiting friends for a New Years celebration, and with a day or two on my own, thought it would be a great opportunity to attempt to start that story which had been buzzing around my head.

On the 4th of May 2019 I hit publish on that book. Originally titled Kathmandu, and now re-titled Kathmandu Killers, I spent over 18 months working on it.I was, and remain to this day, really proud of it.

By the way, that version or Kathmandu in its original form is still available (should you be interested). You can only get it from my website, though: <u>www.lukerichardsonau thor.com/kathmanduoriginal</u>

It's strange to think back over everything that has changed in that time. In 2017 I was still a high school English teacher, waking up early to write my books in the mornings before school. Now (in 2024 as I update this book) I'm lucky enough that this is a job. I've released several books, hadnumerousAmazon Bestseller tags, and (most importantly) connected with so many adventure lovers (like you).

I'll say that again, because it's important. I can say with

certainty, without doubt, a one-hundred-percent iron clad factoid from planet fact, that the thing I've loved most about this big author experiment is connecting with readers like you. Thank you for picking up my books. Thank you for your reviews, and comments. Thank you for being here.

What the future holds for me, Leo or Allissa, I don't know. As you'll have realized, I've left the series open so that I can revisit it in the future if the inspiration strikes. I've got so many ideas about possible adventures for them.

In the meantime... I want you to know that although the words here are my own, the characters, experiences and some of the events described are wholly inspired by the people I've traveled beside.

If we ever shared noodles from a street-food vendor, visited a temple together, played cards on a creaking overnight train, or had a beer in a back-street restaurant, you are forever in this book, and for that, I thank you too!

Again, thank you for coming on the adventure with me. I hope to see you again.

Luke

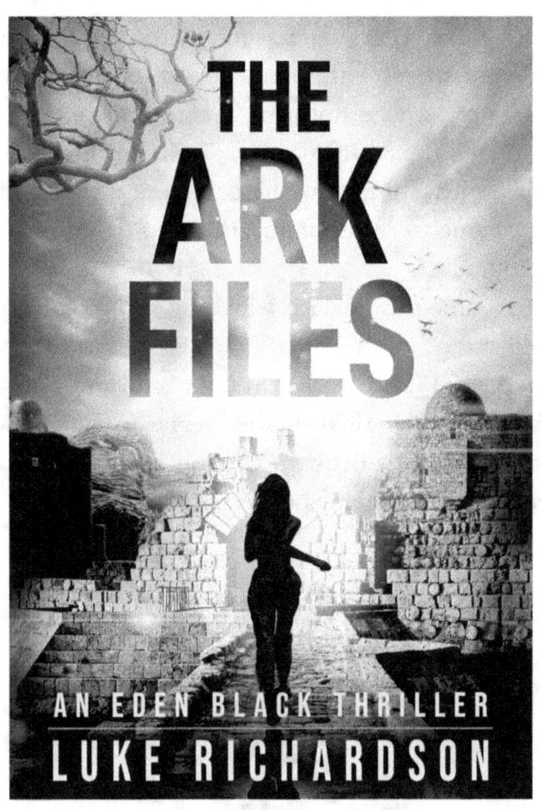

A secret society...
An ancient manuscript...
One woman to save the world...

Professional treasure hunter EDEN BLACK is no stranger to action. After all, the artifacts she spends her life returning to their rightful owners aren't always easy to access.

When Eden's father dies in a plane crash, her life's turned upside down. Grief turns to fear when she learns that it wasn't an accident. Everyone involved in an archaeological dig twenty years ago has met with a similar untimely end. Everyone that is, but Eden who was ten at the time.

When her father's house is raided and burned to the ground, Eden's forced into action. To learn the truth about her father's death and save herself from sharing his fate, Eden must uncover the manuscript and expose its secrets once and for all.

But this time the world is watching, and not everyone is on her side.

THE ARK FILES is the first in a brand-new pulse-pounding archaeological thriller series by Luke Richardson. Fans of Dan Brown, Clive Cussler, and Ernest Dempsey will devour this in hours!

www.lukerichardsonauthor.com/arkfiles

Or search your local Amazon store, your favourite bookseller, or ask in your local library for **The Ark Files by Luke Richardson.**